A Song of Four Marías

By
Adele Nova O'Neill
&
Elizabeth Stone O'Neill

Great Owl Press

© 2021 Great Owl Press & Adele Nova O'Neill

ISBN 978-8-9891441-0-5
First Printing 2023 by Great Owl Press
Front Cover Photo: Adele Nova O'Neill
Cover Design Kyle Lechner (clevercreature.net)

This is a work of fiction, although set in Stockton, California in the early 1960s, names, characters, businesses, events, and incidents are either products of the authors' imaginations or are used in a fictitious manner. Any resemblance to actual persons, living or dead, or actual events is purely coincidental.

Printed in the United States of America
1. Young Adult 2. Historical Novel 3. Coming-of-Age 4. Romance 5. LatinX

Books may be purchased in quantity and/or special sales by contacting the publisher:

GREAT OWL PRESS
Editor: Adele Nova O'Neill
7445 Andrea Ave.
Stockton, California 95207
www.greatowlpress.com
greatowlpress@gmail.com

ALSO BY ELIZABETH STONE O'NEILL

Great
Owl
Press

NONFICTION

Meadow in the Sky: A History of Yosemite's Tuolumne Meadows Region (Revised and updated by Adele Nova O'Neill)
Tioga Tramps: Day Hikes in the Tioga Pass Region (with John Carroll O'Neill, revised and updated by Adele Nova O'Neill)
Mountain Sage: The Life Story of Carl Sharsmith, Yosemite's Famous Ranger/Naturalist (revised and updated by Adele Nova O'Neill)

POETRY AND FICTION

Leaky Borders: The Mexican Poems
Heart Cutters: The Wonderful and Terrible Chronicle of the Aztec Invasion of Iberia (with Adele Nova O'Neill)

Little Owl
Books
FOR CHILDREN

LITTLE OWL CHILDREN'S BOOKS

Tuolumne—How the Runny River Ran
Kai's Dinosaurs
The Beautiful World

LITTLE OWL BILINGUAL BOOKS FOR CHILDREN

1.   *Papá y el Bandido* Spanish/English
2.   *Una Sorpresa para Juan y Rosa* Spanish/English
3.   *¡ Viva Mamá !* Spanish/English
La Serie del Bandidos: The Bandit Series (Boxed Set of Books 1-3)
4.   *El Mundo Hermoso* Spanish/English
piphoplok da srasa saat The Beautiful World Khmer/English

DEDICATION

**This book is dedicated to my mother,
Elizabeth Stone O'Neill,
Who started this book but did not live
to see it finished.**

**And to
All the Chicana girls**

**in both of our classes over many years of teaching
who told us their stories,
who faced challenges similar to the ones in this book.**

But this is a work of fiction.

I want to thank the members of my writing critique group whose input has been invaluable in making me a better writer.

Pam Van Allen
Alysse Adularia
Harlan Hague
Dan Hobbs
Betsy Keithcart
Mariah Parke

A Song of Four Marías
A Novel

By
Adele Nova O'Neill
&
Elizabeth Stone O'Neill

A Song of Four Marías

CONTENTS

THE FOUR MARÍAS

Let me alone! Let—Me—Alone! My whole life pounding through me and through all of us. I've got to carry it with me forever. We all got to carry it forever. I don't know if I'm strong enough, cause I got to carry them too. And them me.

The Four Marys they called us—but we said The Four Marías. Who loved each other.

And it's pounding like a gong. Gone! Gone! Gone!

And now we three that is left, we got to go on with our lives.

CHAPTER ONE
MARÍA PEREZ: AMIGAS

We started being friends about fifth grade just like any other bunch of girls. Well, not exactly, because we were Mexicans. That's what *they* called us, but our families say *Chicanas*.

We had no idea one of us would die the way she did, and the rest of us weren't there to help her.

I read the song that María Rendón wrote before she did it. It was with a wad of papers María Jiménez's brother snitched from her room after the police took her body away. He was always snitching stuff.

We read her song together, and we all cried.

CHAPTER TWO
MARÍA GUTIERREZ: GOD'S WILL

Up until María Rendón done what she done to herself, I could think of only three other bad things happened in my life. I mean, really bad things, not just cut fingers or stubbed toes.

The first was when the twins was born, but I will tell you about that later.

After that comes when my dog got runned over by a car and died there on the curb. I cried like everything. I was just a little kid, but I still remember, and it still hurts.

The third bad thing was when my *abuelita* died, my grandmother, you know. She was always real kind to me and give me things. Like when I was sick, she made tea out of some stuff she bought from a Mexican store-man. It tasted bad, but it made me well. She done things like that.

She was real old and wore a shawl on her head and had only one tooth hanging down in her mouth. When she died, I cried and cried. My mom said it's all right, she's in heaven. When they had the rosary, I didn't even want to go, and I stayed home and just cried. But I don't want to talk about it. After she was gone, I didn't have such good times no more.

The worst bad thing was what happened to María Rendón. I didn't understand then, and my mother wouldn't talk about it. Nobody talked about it to me, but it seemed like everybody talked about it to theirselves. It was almost like she hadn't died because she never lived. In a way it's worse because of all the hush-hush.

I think María Pérez and María Jiménez knew more about it than me. But if I knew more, it might hurt worse. There's things you rather not know sometimes. Like I don't always want to know where Félix is. He's my husband, and I just wouldn't want to know any bad thing he done.

It's a lie to say I couldn't understand about María Rendón. I did understand, the way you understand the shape of something you see in the dark. Not all the light places, not all the lines and curves. Still, you know something is there, and you know if something is coming at you.

I understood like in the dark, after watching María and Pedro for years. No, not watching. That sounds like I was waiting for something to happen. And I wasn't. I never thought anything special would happen. They were what they were. Theirselves. After all, I'm me, and I don't want nobody should follow after me with no spyglass, saying, okay, what next? I didn't do that to them, neither.

Anyways, we grew up together and sometimes she was my best friend. Her and María Jiménez and María Pérez. Honest, I couldn't really say which one was my best friend. Though for some time now I haven't seen much of María Jiménez, and you know why.

But now after it's all over and looking back, I can see the shape of things much clearer than I could at the time. I can't say I can see how it happened, but I sort of feel it.

Gosh, I can't even remember when we started being friends. It must of been about fifth grade because that's when we moved into Lever Village. That's a subdivision south of Stockton, in California in case you don't know. They have pretty nice houses, and they'll take us Mexicans with no questions, and colored people and Filipinos and black people too. Some of the houses are public housing for people on welfare, but my dad built ours. He didn't like to spend that much money on a house. He's sort-of, well, you'd call him tight. Because every cent he makes, he likes to save for going back to Mexico. He says we're going back there to live when he gets enough, and he'll be a rich man in Mexico.

It's funny, me saying "we," because now that me and Félix are married, I guess we'll stay here. He's from Mexico too, like my dad, but he don't want to go back. He don't want to be poor like he was there, sometimes not having enough to eat even, or having to borrow money for the funeral if somebody died. I'll tell you later about me and Félix getting married.

But about my dad and mom, they come from Mexico before I was born. They had one baby already, but my *tía* in Mexico, my aunt I mean, had nobody to live with, so they left the baby with her to raise. Or maybe because they wanted him to stay in Mexico and be Mexican. Just like they want for all their kids. Only I guess now me and Félix are American. Maybe though, when my dad and mom go back and get a house there, me and Félix might go back too. I think I'd like that.

My sister Anna went down to visit my *tía* in Mexico, and she says it's nice. The flowers in the garden smell sweet, and she got to wear pretty dresses, and they walk around the *plaza* in the evening. She liked our brother, too. She says he's a real Mexican, handsome and all.

So anyways, my dad and mom must of been young then, only having one baby, who they left there, and they come up to Texas. Of course, they didn't have no car, so they got a ride a ways with some men they knew, and after a while they walked. They didn't have no good shoes, just sandals like they wear down there. When the sandals fell apart, my dad said they couldn't go to the United States barefoot, so they spent their last money on getting the sandals sewed up, and they didn't get nothing to eat that night, but they come in with shoes on.

Of course, after they lived here a while, they didn't use those old *huaraches* no more but got store-bought shoes instead.

My dad worked in the fields at first and my mom with him. They don't talk much about it. But pretty soon I was born, and my mom used to carry me out to the field and lay me in the shade. She'd pay some kid that was there to watch the baby so she could work with my dad. Maybe it was topping onions or in the potatoes, or in the fall they went to the plums or the peaches.

It was bad when there was no field work, but my dad was funny about going on welfare. He said he had no use for the American government and that "damn Johnson," and as long as he had two hands to work, he would spit in the eye of anybody that give him something for nothing. So, he made my mother go hungry instead of asking for help.

I don't understand that, because everybody has to go on welfare sometimes. Like this winter Félix couldn't get nothing, and he went on welfare, but he was ashamed to tell my dad. I think my dad would of throwed us both out. So, every day Félix would go out away from the house like he was working, so my dad wouldn't know.

Maybe that's where the trouble between me and Félix started because he didn't have nothing to do, and he couldn't stay home with me, so he'd go out with some other fellows. Maybe they'd go to a cock fight or I don't know what. But they would just bum around with a bottle, and when he come home real late, he would be drunk. Of course, I couldn't do nothing about it. I couldn't tell my dad to keep an eye on Félix, cause then he'd know we was on welfare. And even when Félix beat me, I had to not holler, or my folks would get to thinking he was drunk. Which he was. Then they would ask did he drink on his job all the time or what?

So, I just had to take it. But I can tell you I was glad when the asparagus started in the spring, and Félix got to working again, and we didn't have to be ashamed in front of my folks, and he bought me new dresses and things.

Only it wasn't the same as before because he still had these friends, so he still goes out at night and comes back stinking of whiskey. I thought when the baby come it'd be different, especially if it was a boy, because then he'd be proud to have a son and maybe stay home sometimes.

Oh, I hoped it was a boy! I prayed every day for a boy. I even went to a *curandera*. She said she couldn't do much, but she give me some dried flowers to make tea out of. She said it might help, if there wasn't no *bruja* working charms against me.

It cost me five dollars, and the tea tasted bad, like things my grandmother use to make for me. But I didn't care as long as I got a boy. I told Félix I paid the five dollars to the doctor. Generally, he don't care much about religion or things like that. But I wasn't sure how he'd take it, so I told him a lie instead of risking trouble. He wanted me to have the baby in the hospital. He said it's the American way.

That made my dad mad, because he says all of us was born at home with a lady to help, and American hospitals would kill the mothers and switch the babies. I thought that was silly, but now I don't know.

I know when my mother was carrying my little brother, she must of got scared or something. She kept bleeding, and she asked my dad if maybe she should try the real doctor. But he wouldn't let her. He paid the midwife a lot of money, and she brought all kinds of things to set around my mother's bed, and I don't know what all she done, because they wouldn't let me in. But if anything could of saved my little brother, I guess she would of.

When my little brother died just after he was born, my mother cried and cried. We kept him in the house in a box all night, and my mother cried all that night. It was a scary night. My dad told my mother not to cry because it was God's will, and the baby was in heaven now and would never have to go through all the sorrows of life but was already a angel right now.

That was the only boy my folks ever had, except my brother in Mexico that I never saw.

I guess it was God's will, all right. Because everything that happens is God's will. Only if she had of gone to the hospital, maybe the baby would of lived, and wouldn't that of been God's will too? How can God have two wills?

Gosh, if you call everything that happens God's will, then wouldn't you just lay down and let everything happen, and never do nothing?

Like maybe it was God's will for my folks to be born poor in Mexico. But they walked over the border in their old huaraches and look at the way my dad worked at two jobs, one in the day and one at night, so's he can keep saving money to go back and be a rich man in Mexico. I wouldn't dare ask him if that is maybe trying to go against God's will, but it makes you think.

In a lot of ways my dad is different from other people. My mother, for instance, while she does what he says, and saves like he tells her to, she would never think of living that way herself. She wouldn't even mind going on welfare, I think. She said once, about María Rendón's mother being on welfare, when my dad said better starve than take charity—my mother said it's the duty of everybody to help everybody, and if you don't have it what's wrong with getting it from them that does?

My dad got so worked up about that he called her a damn fool woman and went away for a few hours.

He never goes off and gets drunk like Félix, but maybe he just goes for a walk on the levee.

This time when he come back, he wasn't mad no more, but he was acting sort of funny. I mean, he come in and sat down at the table and told us all to come and sit too. We was scared. He looked like he'd been crying.

We all sat down though, Anna and Yolanda and Margarita, and my mom holding my little sister Pilar. That was before Cristina was born. Then my dad started to talk. He started out real quiet and gentle, and after a while he was crying. When he cried, we all cried too because we never seen him cry before. It was awful serious. He was talking Mexican of course, because we never talk nothing but Mexican at home.

He told us about his life. It was awful, really. About how his mother and father had this little house in some town, I can't remember the name of it, and how his father had bees and they used to sell the honey, but they kept the wax to make candles for the Virgin. They didn't have no other children, just him. And they was poor, but they made these beautiful candles.

Somehow, I don't understand it, but there was a law you couldn't make these candles no more, only his folks kept making them anyway, and they sold them secretly to other people, and they used to burn them at night and pray to the Virgin that she would kill the bad people.

Only one night some of these bad people come and took my dad's mother and father away. He was only six years old then, and he seen them go, but they left him behind.

When the people come, his mother was praying, and they kicked over the little altar with the clay Virgin that his mother had, and the candles and the Virgin got all broke up. My father cried, but then in the dark he set up the altar again, and he put the broken candles in front of it, but he couldn't find no match to light them. He wanted to pray, but he got scared and jumped back on his mat where he was sleeping on the floor and pulled his *serape* up over his head. He stayed all alone in the house that night.

He must of gone to sleep because when he woke up it was hot daylight, but he was still alone. He went running out down between the houses to the plaza, and a lot of people was standing there crying. And in the middle of the plaza his mother and father was laying, and they was dead with their eyes open and flies on their faces.

When my dad told us this, he was crying with tears running down, and Anna and Margarita and Yolanda was crying, but then he banged his hand on the table, and we was as quiet as rocks. He wasn't crying no more, but his face got dark and hard.

"Hush," he said, "No more crying. I am a man, and I am ashamed that I cry. But these was holy tears,

tears for the only people that ever loved me. The rest of the world is bad! Evil! Mother-killers! Hard hearts! Charity? Hah! There ain't no charity in this world."

We stared at him, and I didn't hardly breathe. Even my mother looked scared. He went on talking.

"You, *m'hijitas*, daughters mine, have never known these things. But I went hungry then, and I walked in the dark; I ate clay to fill my stomach. I slept in garbage. I grew strong and hard. I am a man now. A man don't cry, except for his dead mother with flies on her face. Only for that.

"So, I took it in my head like this. I will leave this filthy country, and I will go to another filthy country that is richer. Yes, I will be a rich man. Then I will go back to Mexico and build a tombstone for my mother and father. It will have candles of stone and a Virgin on it you can't break. And I won't never take no charity because when I needed help, no man and no woman lifted up a finger to help me, and I won't never ask again."

After that he went out to walk again, and none of us said nothing. We just went to bed. And I cried in bed. I thought of my father walking on the levee in the dark, thinking of his mother laying dead in the plaza. All of a sudden, I felt sorry for my father, like he was still that little boy. I thought, "I would of give him something to eat, not clay." I never felt the same about my father since that day.

It's true I let Félix ask for the welfare because I think my mother is right, and why not accept what the government gives when you need help? Only I couldn't tell my father ever. He wouldn't never understand. And I wouldn't tell my mother, because then she would have to lie to my father for me.

But it's sure hard sometimes knowing what to do.

I asked my mother another time, why didn't the people of that town help my father? Like here in Stockton when Pilar Martínez went out of her head and tried to kill her kids, the neighbors took them and kept them until the people from the county come and said they had to go to the Children's Home. Those poor little kids! I think that was awful, taking them off to the children's home where nobody really cared about them. The county people said they wasn't getting good food at Miz López's house, and they was dirty. But what's dirt if you have other kids in the bed with you, and plenty of tortillas and peppers? My dad says he's proud to eat tortillas, and the Americans can have that cotton stuff they call bread. I think he's right. But at the Children's Home they have bread.

Anyway, when I asked my mother why the people didn't help my father after his folks was killed, she said she didn't know, but maybe they was scared. But then she said my father run away and hid.

The big thing is, he thought they wouldn't help him. From that he got to hating them and hating the world.

But he's pretty good to my mother. He would never say he thinks a lot of her, of course, but I notice he's never mean to her like some husbands. He never beat her, even like Félix has been known to beat me. My mother is a lucky woman, even if she don't get to spend as much as some people, because my dad don't hardly ever get drunk. He is too stingy to spend the money on booze, but it don't make no difference why. The thing is, that he don't do it. From what I seen, drinking leads to fighting, and going to jail, or getting in trouble in some way, and trouble leads to drinking, and it goes around and around.

I wish Félix wouldn't drink. But he is my husband, and I can't say nothing to him about it, or he would be really mad. And it is true, he don't drink so much when he's working. If only he could work all year around, I think it would be a lot better. But you can't ask the crops to grow so's there's work all year. You can't pick tomatoes in January, not even if that's when you need the work the worst, no matter what. God's will again, I guess.

But I started to tell you about when we was kids, me and Pedro and María Rendón and María Jiménez and María Pérez. My folks call me María, and Félix does too. But at school, the teachers called me Mary, and so did the kids. Like they couldn't say María. So, in my class they called us The Four Marys. Almost like a club. Pedro was María Rendón's brother, so he was always around too. But he wasn't part of the club because boys can't be friends to girls the same way girls can.

Boys and girls are so different from each other, I think it's funny that we're all human beings. We look different, and act different, and we sure think different. My dad says it's crazy for us to go to school with boys because we should learn different things. I think maybe he's right. Maybe that's why they didn't mind me marrying Félix, because then I quit school. And my dad never did like my being in high school with boys. If he could of afforded it, he'd of rather I went to Catholic school. But that costs a awful lot, especially if you have six girls like my folks do, though they do charge less for big families. My dad said when I got married that now I should stay home and act like a woman, not like a crazy American teenager. And that's what I try to do.

I don't think I ever acted so crazy, though. Even back in fourth and fifth grades, and after that, I never got to go to other people's houses after school or things like that. I had to go straight home to help out. Especially if my mother was working. Lots of times I would stay out of school to babysit, since I was the oldest. It's a good thing they're all girls, because they minded me pretty good. But if they was boys, I would of had a awful time, because boys hate to do what their sisters say, even if the sister is older. So, I was really lucky having all sisters, excepting my brother in Mexico who I never saw and my baby brother that died. My dad doesn't like having all girls, and my mother doesn't either. But it was easier for me. I liked looking after the kids. And I couldn't wait until my baby was born. But I hoped it would be a boy. I thought, I will have something to do then, for when Félix ain't home. Of course, even now that I am married, I still watch my sisters a lot for my mother. But even baby Cristina is getting bigger, and she'll be babysitting herself pretty soon. I need a family of my own.

So, when I was helping so much at home, the other Marías would come over after school. Their mothers let them go out more than mine done. My mother says look at María Jiménez, and that proves what happens when you give a girl too much freedom. But then look at María Pérez. She had even more freedom than María Jiménez, and she never got in no trouble and is as nice a girl as you could know.

But then, she loved Pedro from when we was kids. And he didn't love her. That keeps a person out of trouble, don't it?

María Jiménez was another matter. But I don't care what anybody says, I will always love that girl. She is not only good looking, which is no reason to like her, but she has a kind of goodness under all the badness.

If I was laying in a ditch, and she come by — there's a story in the Bible about something like this, I think — María Jiménez would drag me out of there with her own hands, and she would do everything for me. You got to remember that even living like she does and taking money for — things no girl is supposed to take money for — it's partly to help her family.

Oh, she talks tough. But there's another thing too. She never loved nobody like I love Félix. You can say all you want about him. But when he is nice, he is really nice, and he is my husband, so why shouldn't I admit that I love him? When he comes home, I am so glad. And maybe it ain't nice to say, but he really does thrill me, too. I just wish he was home oftener.

I was going to tell you about how we got to know each other, and it happened this way. I would never let my folks know all about it, but this is the truth of how it happened.

We was in the third year at Edison High, and I used to walk with sometimes one person, sometimes another. But always one of the Marías, and maybe Pedro would be along. If Pedro wasn't in school — like working in the fields or something — Juan Soto would walk with us. But never the two at the same time, because Juan was sure afraid of Pedro. Juan had always liked María Rendón a little, and he knew Pedro would never stand for it. Pedro never grew up that way, I mean to get interested in other girls except his sister. Though he was friends to María Pérez, but not in what you could call a romantic way.

So, we had a pretty long walk across the fields. I never walked alone. I was sort of afraid, there was so many colored kids and white kids that would tease me. Of course, I knew some of these kids since being little, and some of them were not bad, but still I felt better if I had my friends. And like my dad says, Mexicans should stick to Mexicans and not go mixing with other people because only bad comes from things like that.

In those fields they used to grow just grass and cut it in the spring. And in the winter, there was a old guy with a big lot of goats, that stood out there day after day. He was Mexican, but there was something wrong with him. I mean, his head was a funny shape, and he couldn't talk right. He would just lean on his stick, and wave to us kids when we went by. I would of been afraid of him if I had not had my friends with me.

This one year when it was first fall, I mean just after the rains started and the wild mustard was coming up, and long before the dust started to blow, there was this big boy who was always out helping the old goat herder, whose name I don't know. The boy was Félix, but I didn't know that then. Only he would smile when we went by. I guess he didn't know we could talk Mexican. One day María Jiménez, who was kind of nervy, said, "*Buenos días*," and he answered back fast enough. After that every day he would say that to us. And one thing led to another. We found out he had came for a *bracero*, but when the season was over, and he was supposed to go back to Mexico, he didn't want to go. His folks in Mexico was dead, he told us, and it's true because he never seems to want to go back there or have nobody to go back to. So, he started living with this old man in his shack and helping him with his animals. And being from Mexico, he didn't even know how poor he was, because this was just like he had always lived, with not too much to eat and his clothes all mended and patched. The old man is too dumb to know how poor he is, either, even though he has lived here a long time. So, they got along just fine.

Félix would talk to María Jiménez because she would talk back to him, but he told me later she was too American for him. And María Pérez never took no interest to talk to him. And Pedro and María Rendón—well, Félix thought they was *novios*, not brother and sister. And that left me.

I guess that even if I never spoke to him, Félix could tell I liked him from the beginning. And with my pigtails which my folks wouldn't let me cut, I seemed more like the kind of girl he had known. Anyway, he wouldn't speak to me, neither, but when he was talking to María Jiménez, he would be looking at me.

"He likes you a awful lot," María Jiménez told me. And just her saying that made me feel hot all over. And that made me feel even shyer because I was afraid he would know. I guess he did too.

It got so that the others would walk on ahead when we crossed the field, and then Félix would come up and talk to me a little bit. I never answered much. But he would smile, and I liked his smile.

I am sort of clumsy when I get embarrassed, and one day when he was standing there waiting for me, I got so mixed up I stumbled. And quick as anything he jumped over and picked me up. I didn't need that much help, but there we was standing in the field, him with his hands on my arms, and I begun to tremble from head to foot. No man ever had ahold of me like that before, and I was half frightened and wanted to cry, but at the same time I thought I would die if he let go of me. And my friends had walked ahead and was way far away, and if they seen they didn't let on.

"María," Félix said, "María, you marry me!"—We was speaking Mexican, because he didn't know no English then.

And I kept shaking and didn't answer. And then he kissed me.

This kiss—it wasn't like nothing that ever happened to me before. I have been to the movies but not too often. And I have seen other kids kissing, but I never knew it was like it was. I couldn't believe it.

It was like the feel of needles and pins and lilacs and roses. No, it was like music, some kind of church music that got faster and turned to a dance. No, it was like being put in the spin-dryer and whirled around until the world disappeared, and there was only stars—great big ones coming at me.

Oh, I don't know how to say it. Either you know what I mean or you don't. I just leaned my head on Félix's shoulder, and I said, "*Sí*, Félix, sí." It happened just as fast as that.

I didn't go to school that day. I just walked out of the field with Félix, and he took me down to the levee. Well, I can't tell you all about that. We hid for three days in the bushes, and then we went back to my folks.

They was a little bit mad, but it blew over. They liked Félix and him being from Mexico. We moved into their house, and that's where we are now.

CHAPTER THREE
MARÍA JIMENEZ: PADRINO'S GIFT

Me and María Rendón was always friends, though I will say she was kind of odd. Her and her brother Pedro, I mean. They always—well, there was that time Pedro got hit by a ball and it was María that cried. I mean, I like my brother but man! If he got hit by a ball, I'd laugh. I'd say it served him right for the way he treated me.

But with María and Pedro it was so different it was funny. When we had folk dancing in school and Miz Arthur'd get mad and her face would get all red at the kids cutting up, and I used to hate it because the boys was always shorter—only George Alvarado was cute anyway—when we was dancing in the gym, Pedro wouldn't dance with nobody but his sister, and she wouldn't dance with nobody but Pedro.

Do you think it was because of their being so close, the way things turned out? I mean, why would María of done what she done, if what her mom says is the truth? María Pérez believes it, and from what Pedro said to me, I guess I believe it too. And come to think of it, María Pérez was in love with Pedro the whole time. Everybody knowed it except Pedro, even his sister knowed. And even though she was so crazy about Pedro her own self, she didn't get mad at María Pérez, but I guess that's because she knowed Pedro wouldn't look at nobody but her anyhow.

The first time I ever seen them, Pedro and María I mean, they was just moving in next door to us. We seen them coming with all this stuff, but it was real broken-up junk with wheels and chair legs sticking out under the canvas tied over the top of the U Haul Trailer, and we seen it was this man driving and this fat woman and two skinny kids sitting in back. They didn't speak to nobody, and I think the man was drunk, the way he stopped the car with such a big jerk and the kids both fell off the back seat and the girl cried, and that was María. She got a bloody nose. And then the woman start screaming in Mexican, what did he think he was doing? And right there sitting in the car he hauled off and hit her across the face and broke her nose, and then he went in the house, and we didn't see him no more.

So, there was María yelling in the back seat and the mother up front with blood streaming out of her nose. I think he broke a tooth too. He must of hit her awful hard. She yells, "Pedro," and Pedro sticks his head up over the back seat, and she yells again, "Pedro!" But she don't say no more, so Pedro climbs over the seat with a dirty rag he's got, and he starts mopping his mother's face just like she's a doll or something, and he starts crying while he does it, and she's crying and María's crying, only when she sees all the blood she stops for a minute, and then she cries all the harder. By this time her nose has stopped bleeding and she just has these bloody streaks down over her chin and spots on her dress. But it has got so many spots already it don't make much difference.

My mother has been sitting on the porch watching all this with my *Nina*, and keeps saying, don't go mixing up in it, but my mother can't stand seeing that little boy crying and mopping his mother's face, so she goes running out. Nina tries to stop her, but my mother shoves her back on the porch, where Nina starts laughing because it is sort of funny. My Nina's like that. Maybe a little cracked. The sight of blood makes her laugh. I think it's account of the bruja, the witch that killed Nina's son by sticking pins in a doll. When they found him dead was when Nina started laughing at the sight of blood, so you can tell it was the bruja. Everybody knows who the bruja is, but they're scared to name her.

Anyway, my mom jerks open the car door and says to come over and wash up at our house. The lady gets up with blood all down her front and even on her shoes, and she's holding her nose and crying still, and she walks in the house with María and Pedro hanging back behind her. They wouldn't talk none. We got her all cleaned up, and my mother took her to the clinic in our car, but first she had to lend her a clean dress of Nina's. By the time the blood was all cleared up Nina stopped laughing. It's only when there's blood. So, us kids and María and Pedro stayed home, and Miz Rendón got her nose bandaged up at the hospital, but it's looked kind of crooked ever since. Nina cooked tacos for us, and we had beans, but María and Pedro wouldn't eat much and wouldn't talk much. When my mother and their mother come back, Miz Rendón said she wasn't going to sleep in no bed with no nose-breaker, and anyway he was drunk, so we made beds for them on the kitchen floor, and we hooked all the screens in case he tried to get in during the night, but nothing happened that time.

The next morning my mother sent me and my sister Rosalva to see if he was still there, and the door was open and there wasn't much of anything left in the house, and the man was gone. He must of took off real early, with the car and everything. Miz Rendón didn't have no pots or nothing to cook with, so my mother give her some of ours.

Her and my mother was real good friends most of the time. Once in a while they'd go to it and have a awful fight. Like one time my mother called her fat, and she said my mother was just *flaca*, weak and skinny. Of course, she is fat, and my mother is skinny, but anyways my mother said maybe she was flaca but she could hit hard, and she socked Miz Rendón in the stomach, and Miz Rendón jumped on her and pulled her hair. My sister Carla come out and hit her behind with a board, and she jumped up and run in the house screaming. But she didn't call the police, because she was afraid she'd get turned out of the house, being as how it's public housing, and she was afraid of losing her welfare money too.

She went on welfare after her husband left that time, and when she got her checks, she bought a lot of stuff. But she never could make the money go to the end of the month. Seems like she couldn't count or something. They never had enough to eat at the end, and if she and my mother wasn't mad, she'd come over and ask for some beans or something, and my mother always give it to her.

My mother says she ain't never going on welfare even if she has to steal, and to tell you the truth sometimes she does—just shoplifting and things like that. She says half the world is cats and half is rats, and she won't be no rat.

I got to hand it to my mother, she has ten kids and we never had to go hungry like María and Pedro Rendón. When my dad was out of work, my mother just yakked at him to get work, and if he didn't, or even if he did, she'd go out and work herself. Sometimes she took me, like packing potatoes, and we'd ride back on the bus with all the braceros, all men and just my mother and me. They talked to her in Mexican, and she'd laugh, but they scared me. I didn't know too much Mexican, but sometimes it seemed like she'd make a date or something with some of them.

One of the worst times in our family was one time my father was out of work. He cut his foot topping onions, and it got all swole up, and he couldn't work or even walk on it. He wouldn't go to the doctor. He's from Mexico, not like my mother. She come from Los Angeles. But she couldn't get him to go, so she said okay she'd go out and work. Her and me went around trying to find work, but it seemed like there wasn't none. I was pretty small then. She wouldn't leave me home with my dad because he'd just lay there and drink, and when he's drunk his face gets red and he gets real mean. Why, one time when he was drunk, he beat me with his belt until my back was bleeding. Anyways, she took me with her. It was at night, and we went to this camp. She told me to go sit on the steps and wait for her, and she went inside.

She was gone a long time. I could hear people talking and laughing, but I didn't dare move because she told me to stay there. It got real cold on the steps, and the mosquitoes was biting my legs. After a while my mother come out. She said come on, and we walked down the road to the bus stop and got the bus home. We had to wait a long time, and she wouldn't talk to me or nothing.

It was pretty late when we got home, and my dad was laying on the couch with his foot up, and his eyes was real red, and the bottle was empty. He jumped up at my mother like he was a cat. "I know where you was," he's yelling at her in Mexican, and he grabs her purse and opens it up, and takes out a handful of dollar bills. He throws them all over the floor, and he grabs her by the throat.

"You whore!" he's shouting, and she's trying to get loose and her face is getting red. He shakes her back and forth like a rag. I got real scared at that and run over to Miz Rendón's house, and she called the police for me. Then I just stood looking across at my house, and hearing my father shouting and a lot of scuffling, and I am scared to go over until the police car comes, which it does pretty fast. All the other kids has run over with me, so it's just my mom and dad left in the house.

I didn't see just what happened, but the next thing they are carrying my father out, and he is crying, "Teresa, don't let them take me to jail." Then I am surprised at my mother because she comes out and says, "No, don't take him."

They set him down on the ground, and the cop argues with her, and she stands there like not knowing what to do, but he goes on crying so she says again, "That's all right, don't take him." So, they just leave him laying there on the grass, after the cop says, "Okay, lady, it's your funeral."

My father is too heavy for my mother to carry him in, and he's too drunk to walk. But he rolls over and sort of crawls into the house and flops on the couch and falls asleep.

After he is snoring, my mother picks up all the dollar bills and hides them in the bottom of the bean bag. I know where she hides her money, but nobody else does. For sure my father will never look in the beans. One thing about my mother, she didn't never accept no charity, and she always earned her own way in the world.

My dad went out the next day after he got sober, and he didn't come back till late that afternoon. He come back with a friend in his friend's car. My mom was in the kitchen making enchiladas, and he didn't say nothing to her. He just called my little brother Stefan that was only about two years old and was playing on the porch. "Come on, Stefan, *vamos* bye-bye," he said. My mother didn't want Stefan to go with him, but she couldn't do nothing about it.

My dad didn't come back for dinner, and we ate all the enchiladas. Real late, he brought Stefan, and Stefan had scratches and cuts all over his face and body and was crying. He dumped him on the porch and took off again. Stefan couldn't talk, he just whimpered, and my mom went out and got him, and she give him a bath in the kitchen sink, and she cried all the time. She cried all night long. She kept Stefan in the bed with her that night, and even after he went to sleep, I could hear my mother crying. But when my dad come back the next day, she didn't say nothing to him about it, and he didn't say nothing neither. He just asked her for five dollars, and she give it to him, and he went off and bought a couple of bottles of gin and come back again.

By this time his foot was better, and he went back to work, and they patched it up. That was the worst fight they ever had. My mom never took me back to the camp again, and I don't know if she went there herself, because after that for a long time my father had work. Like I say, at our house there was always enough to eat.

A funny thing was about my dad and mom getting married. Most kids have not seen their parents get married, but I have.

He's not really my father, because my mother had me first. She was living at home with her folks then. She had me, and she had my brother Stefan. Then her brothers said they would get her a man. So, they took this trip to Mexico to look for someone.

They was driving along in Mexico, I don't know where it was, and they give this man a lift in their car. Then when they come to the town where he lived, he asked them to have a drink with him. Then they all had a drink together. Then my uncles told him how they was looking for a man for their sister, and he said,

"How about me?" So, he come back with them to the States, and that's how my father and mother got married.

Well, not really married, but they had all the kids. Then one time they got the idea to get married. So, they went to the City Hall and got married. I wasn't at the wedding, but man, what a party we had! The men had beer, and the ladies and kids had soda, and we had tacos and a cake as big as a table-top, and a lot of guys brought Mexican records, and they all danced.

That was one of the good times, but to tell you the truth we had a awful lot of bad times too. Fighting of my mom and dad and not always finding enough money and having to scrounge. My mom showed me how to scrounge out of stores and things like that. I am pretty quick at that and didn't never get caught, which is why I have lots of earrings and things now, and I don't never have to pay for my perfume.

When I used to hang around with the other Marías—they called us The Four Marys, and that was María Gutiérrez and María Pérez and María Rendón and me—that was good. We started about ten or eleven, and we was together all through high school. Or that is, until other things happened. We just stuck together even though we sometimes had our fights. Like María Gutiérrez saying María Rendón stunk, and I thought they would scratch their eyes out, but they made it up. You know how kids is. My brothers and sisters are into it all the time, and as old as I am I get mad and beat them up once in a while, especially Stefan because he talks too much. And my sister Rosalva, she is so lazy and never does nothing to help and tells lies about me. Or even if they are partly true, she oughtn't to go around talking about it.

Later María Gutiérrez run away and got married to Félix Gomez. That was a bad deal, really. It's enough to make you not want to get married at all. Even though I had something to do with it, I will say that.

Then María Pérez got sort of serious, studying all the time and acting like one of the Sisters or something. But I don't mean religious. I think it was account of her being stuck on Pedro. But then, her family was different. I mean, they was never on welfare, and nobody never called the cops on them.

Of course, it was sort of like that with María Gutiérrez's family, too. Some folks seem to have all the luck or something. And María Gutiérrez wasn't stuck up or nothing, which is a good thing, because later she had her own streaks of bad luck and wouldn't of had nothing to be stuck up about.

But how can I hold it against María Pérez, the way she acts? God, if I ever loved anybody like she loves Pedro! We all know it. Pedro knows it. He told me so hisself. Do you know, I think maybe now that his sister's out of the way, maybe he'll look at María Pérez. And between you and me, that would be a good thing.

Well, it's enough to make you sad. Like me. Better looking than any of the others. And not married, and not about to be. The boys always looked at me, only not the right way. Maybe I didn't look at them the right way neither—but they was reasons. Sometimes I feel like the showcase where everybody stops and feels the stuff, but nobody ever buys.

I can honestly tell you I ain't never loved no man. It's easier that way. Would I want to of been María Gutiérrez, home crying with her belly fat and jumping around, cause she didn't know where Félix was? Or María Pérez, just walking around like a ghost, or because she loves a ghost not a real man that will take her and love her? Or maybe like María Rendón— dead?

Hell, no! Maybe I ain't the purest lady in Stockton, but I have my fun too. In my own way. And lots of pretty dresses.

My brother sticks up for me. In fact, when people have called me names, which makes me mad, Stefan says, "Okay, sis, you let me clean them guys up." He says this even though we have had some pretty bad times, and when we was little, we used to fight each other when we wasn't fighting other people. When he got in a fight with some kid I would get in on his side, kicking and scratching like anything. And it was the same with him for me. Only as soon as it was over, we was hitting each other. Man, we fought a lot.

My mom is like that. If somebody has it in for one of us kids, she'll beat the hell out of them. But then she'll turn right around and hit the kid, only not in front of the other person. She's hit me with the broom all over, face and neck and back and everything.

But I can't hold it against her. Honest, I think a lot of my mom. She done the best she could for all of us and having ten kids is no state fair. She says she wants more. But I think she just says that and don't mean it. Because my dad has been staying home and they ain't had too many fights, but I notice she ain't had no babies for a while now. Maybe she knows something to do about it. I could tell her a thing or two about that, but I won't, because her and me never talked about stuff like that, even if I'm grown up now.

There's lots of things we just can't talk about. One is what happened when I was fourteen. I'd die before I'd tell her, even though I think maybe she knows. In a way, I wonder how she let it happen. But from what I seen of her life I guess it didn't seem so bad to her, and now I am giving her money every week I guess she don't mind that too.

But I could never talk to the other Marías about it, as good friends as we have always been. I guess I'm just the bad bean in the bag, but I won't talk about it. And they can take me or leave me.

Christ, I don't really mean that. They was my best friends. I don't know what I do mean, only life is a big card game, and some gets the aces, and some gets the jokers. I got the joker.

I was getting to about my full size and had a good figure, too. I liked the boys, I mean all of them, no special one. And they liked me. But I didn't know too much about things like that, only what I heard, and that was all mixed up.

Then one time my godfather come up from Nogales. I couldn't remember him from before, and when I seen him, I was surprised because I didn't like him. And you are supposed to like your godfather.

This *compadre* was a short sneaky guy with bad teeth and a moustache. He was always smoking cigars. He didn't talk nothing but Mexican, and my Mexican is not so hot. But I can understand it okay.

He made over me a lot and called me his little daughter, and how good looking I was and all. He was one of those men a girl just naturally don't trust. Even if she's only fourteen, she knows they are sneaky, but older people don't see it and say, "Don't be rude to your *padrino*, he's just being friendly to you." And you can't explain.

He took me out in his car to buy ice cream, and when we parked, he started feeling me up to see how I was developing, he said. I was real embarrassed, but when we got home I was ashamed to tell my mother.

I always sleep in the kitchen on a kind of cot thing we sit on in the day. The kitchen is open to the living room, and my mother made a bed for my godfather on the sofa. Then her and the kids went to bed. I went to bed too, and my dad and my godfather and some other men was setting up in the living room drinking beer and playing cards. But even though they made a lot of noise, I went to sleep. Their talk was just a buzzing in my dreams.

I woke up once and seen my godfather standing at the sink drinking a glass of water. I must of woke up when he turned the faucet on. Then he put down the glass and come over and started feeling me again, his hands going pat-pat up and down me on top of the blanket, and I was ashamed to say nothing, but I thought he oughtn't to do it. Then he went out.

I laid there half-scared hoping they'd play cards all night, and I must of gone to sleep again. Because the next I knew it was all dark. And I heard the floor creak.

Then there was those hands patting me again. I was laying on my back. I whispered, "Please go away." But he didn't say nothing. Before I knowed it, he had throwed off the blanket and was pulling up my slip that I sleep in. I tried to sit up, but he pushed me down and put his hand over my mouth.

"Quiet, darling," he said, and he just laid down on top of me. He was naked excepting for his undershirt, and he smelled.

I was scared to death. Nobody ever done this to me before. I tried to push him off, but even though he was a little guy he was awful strong, and he just went on holding his hand over my mouth and pushed hisself into me. It hurt like anything, and I bit his hand with the tears coming out of my eyes. At that he just squeezed my cheeks against my teeth until I whimpered.

"You keep quiet if you know what's good for you," he whispers.

"Okay," I mumble back, though I am still crying.

When he finished, he says, "If you ever tell your mama, I'll cut your throat," and he runs his fingernail across my neck like a knife blade.

"I won't," I whisper back. Then he gets off me and goes back to the sofa.

I hated him so much I wanted to grab a butcher knife and go stick it in his belly, but I was afraid, because I knowed he would hear me getting it out of the drawer. And he was so strong. I was thinking, if I hear him snoring, I'll get the knife. I laid there a long time almost not breathing, thinking of that knife. After a long time, I hear a snore, and then another, like a truck starting up a long ways off. I turn over, but my bed squeaks and the snoring stops.

I listened a long time, but he must of been a light sleeper, cause every time I moved he seemed to hear me. So finally, I thought I had better give up. And in the end, I did go back to sleep.

The next day I was still hurting, and I didn't even want to speak to that man. But he was extra friendly like the day before, and I had to speak polite to him for fear of what my dad would say, him being my padrino.

Then he asked my mother could he take me and buy me a dress.

"I don't need no new dress," I said. But my mother was sort of pushed at my rudeness and said sure, and not to pay no attention to what I said, and I had to go in his car with him again. It was a old beat-up Chevy and greasy-dirty.

We went to the Villa Fair. That's sort of a supermarket department store near Lever Village where they got all sorts of stuff. He bought me a pink dress with nylon ruffles that I will say looked good on me. Then he bought me a milkshake. All that time I wouldn't hardly speak to him, but he acted like he didn't notice.

When we got in the car to go home, he said, kind of wheedling, "That didn't hurt so bad, María."

"It hurt awful bad," I said. But I was glad I got the dress, only I didn't say so.

"The second time it don't hurt so much," he said. But I didn't answer.

Then he took out a ten-dollar bill and showed it to me. "I tell you what," he said, "you do it again with me, and you get this."

I looked at the ten dollars. Nobody never give me so much money. Then I thought, it ain't as bad as cutting asparagus all day, and you don't get that much.

"Here?" I asked.

"No. Tonight. Like last night. And no noise, neither."

I thought about it. "Okay," I said. "But you give me the ten dollars first."

"No," he said. "That comes afterwards."

I was feeling hard and mean inside. I'm that way about money because I never got nothing free. "No," I said. "First, or nothing."

So, it ends up he gives me the ten-dollars first, and that night he come to my bed again. And it was the truth, that time it didn't hurt hardly at all. He was one of them guys that don't take long, and that time I knowed what was coming.

The next day he went back to Nogales, and I hid the money in my box of hair rollers. I was going to buy myself another dress. But then I thought I would take the kids to the fair one day, so I did, and I bought them all kinds of stuff, hot dogs and cotton candy and plastic dolls. We had a ball, them and me.

My mom asked where did I get all that money, and I said mi padrino give it to me. I don't know if she guessed what for he give it, but a godfather is 'sposed to do things for his godchild, so maybe she didn't guess. Only I think she did.

I got to thinking it was a pretty slick way to make money. Only I didn't know how to get started. But then it just sort of started itself.

I am not a bad looking girl, and the boys has been after me a lot, but I always said no. So next time one of them asked me, I just said, "How much you give me?"

He was surprised cause I guess he thought he would get it free, but he says, "Fifty cents." I laughed in his face and asked what does he think I am? Of course, I can't get no ten dollars out of him because he's in school, but we settle for two dollars. Then he tells his friends I will do it for money, and after that I am earning money pretty steady.

The truth is, I got so I get a lot of fun out of it. Only one thing, I am scared to death I will have a baby. So, when women are talking, I listen. Then I hear there's some pills you can take. I feel like a dope, but I go out to the county hospital and say I am getting married. They tell me my husband-to-be should come too. Then I say, he don't speak English and anyways is working and can't come. So finally, they give me the prescription. These pills cost a lot and I have to up my prices, but by this time I got so many customers it's okay.

So that's how I got started, and I was just in high school two years, but I dropped out. It's too much going to school every day and going out every night.

I never exactly tell my folks, but they know, and maybe they don't like it, but they sure like me giving them money every week and buying things for the kids.

Just once my mother says something, why don't I get a job like decent girls? And I don't like to talk back to her, but I ask her what's wrong with the money I give her? She says, nothing, but I will get in trouble one way or another that way. Then I tell her, I don't know no better than I was taught. So she knows I know what kind of a woman she is, or was—I don't know if she still is or not. And she shuts up. My dad never says nothing. I guess he thinks I already gone bad, and it's no use talking about because I can't be good again.

I ask myself about that sometimes. I mean, am I really so bad? Of course, I don't go to church no more, but I never did go much. I would feel like one big fool going to confession every Saturday and telling the padre I got so much from this one and so much from that one, and him telling me to go and sin no more, when both him and me know I will. It's easier to just not go.

But what if I die? What happens then? Sometimes in the night I get scared. Then I pray to the Virgin of Guadalupe, that is María Mother of God—ain't it funny that her and me has the same name? María, I pray, you must know why men want what I got and why, between you and me, I want what they got. And María, I go on, you know I spend most all the money on my brothers and sisters, and give some to my folks, and keep only enough to dress decent for myself. Then

I feel like a even worse fool, talking about things like that to the Blessed Virgin. And I think, why ain't there nobody, not in heaven or earth, that you can talk to about it, that is both wise and good, and at the same time understands about being dumb and bad and about sin? For it sure is a sin. But if God is sposed to forgive sinners, why can't you talk to Him about it? I'm scared, though, that God would be like my dad and just give me the cold shoulder or worse if I tried.

But when all is said and done, this is how I live, and I sometimes think that anybody including God that doesn't like it, it's their tough.

CHAPTER FOUR
MARÍA AND PEDRO RENDON:
THE HOUSE OF COLORED PAPER

I guess there's no one in the world that would understand about me and my brother Pedro. I guess it never happened before to anybody. Or if it did, everybody else just shut up and wouldn't talk, so I don't know about it. And in a way, that's the worst of it. If somebody else loves somebody, well it's sad.

Like María Pérez loving Pedro. It's real sad, and I'd be the first to say it. But with me, I have to just shut up and die, and there won't be nobody write no sad story about us. It makes me feel like dogs, like we was just dogs. And only the two of us know that it wasn't that way.

Where is Pedro now? I can't understand it. He was always there. Now he's gone, and I have to go it alone.

Oh, well, the whole world wouldn't of let me have him, and that's funny because what difference does it make to them anyhow?

The way I feel about Pedro and Pedro feels about me, maybe it was because of how we was kids together, and we used to get drug around from one job to another with our folks. We practically lived in that old Ford that had the upholstery all rubbed off and with rusted spots on it and no floor mat but just the metal that got so hot in the summer. My folks never had no other kids, just us two.

Sometimes I'd hear my father saying to my mother, did she do something to keep from having kids, or why wasn't she like other women? She'd shout out maybe he wasn't like other men. I didn't understand then, and to tell you the truth I don't now, because what can you do to keep from having babies? It must be something bad, from what my father said. Of course, I don't know if he was lying about my mother or what, but he lied about everything else, and she seemed to me like she wouldn't do nothing bad, at least in them days.

Anyways, they would talk like that all the time we was driving from Colorado to Texas or from Texas to California, and Pedro and me would sit in the back seat with all our pans and things and the handles sticking us and my headless doll for hours and hours. My dad didn't like for us to talk, and he'd tell us to keep our damn mouths shut if we started up, so we'd play no-talking games like finger-wrestling, or guessing which hand a bottle cap was in by pointing. Sometimes Pedro would make little toys and things out of grass and string. He was always smart with his hands.

We went to school sometimes, but it got you all mixed up not knowing any of the kids, and we didn't speak too good English neither, which I guess you can tell from the way I talk even now. My folks just talked Mexican, and we learned that first. Only in school nobody wants you to talk Mexican, like it's dirty words or something. Of course, there's bad words in Mexican too, but it seems just as good to me as English. Frankly, I know a lot more bad words in English, but maybe that's because you see them wrote ever'where, so's everybody learns them all. My mother never used any bad words when we was kids, and my father just talked them with other men, not at home, so I don't know them much. Pedro learned them from Dad, but he never told them to me.

Pedro wanted to take care of me and for me to be a lady, and he used to say no no-good bum like dad was ever going to marry me and bloody my nose so long as he could help it. Of course, he wouldn't dare talk that way with my dad around, but it used to make him mad the way dad wouldn't take him around much like other fathers take their sons, so he talked that way when dad was gone.

He was gone most of the time. Lots of times he would be gone on some job and leave us. We would have a lot of tough times until we got on welfare and started getting the check, but then if my dad come back just once and the welfare people heard about it, they would say he was working and take away our check again, even if he never give us any money. So, we got kind of used to eating when we had it and going hungry when we didn't.

Of course, we had some pretty good times too. I don't want you to think it was all bad. Sometimes when Mom got her check, she'd take us out and buy us everything, new clothes from head to foot, shoes and sox and all. It seemed like the new dresses she got me didn't last too long, because by the time the next check come around, I'd need more things. Mom didn't fix things up too much. She just give my old dresses away. We got to think of people that need it worse than us, she'd say. I never could understand how some girls would wear the same dress for a couple of years, like they didn't care about helping nobody else.

The checks was pretty small though, because we always had them hungry days after we run out of money, before the new check come.

It used to make Pedro cry to see me hungry. I guess you won't believe that, because most brothers would swipe the food from their sisters, but Pedro always took care of me. The last tortillas we had he'd give me, and he'd just say, "Aw, I ain't hungry." So, I'd keep one under my pillow, and then later I'd try to give it to him, but he'd make me eat it anyway. Then when I got a little bigger, he found out we could get stuff in the supermarket, and that helped a lot. I'd stand at the corner of the aisle and watch, and he'd stuff his pockets with candy and things, and then we'd walk out. He was pretty smart. He'd be saying he guessed that wasn't the kind of bread ma wanted. They never caught up with us. We'd go to the levee and divvy it up, and it sure tasted good if you hadn't had nothing to eat for a while. It was harder to steal fruit because it's so big, so we mostly took little things we could slip in our pockets. Ma didn't know we done this. I guess she wouldn't of liked it, but maybe she wouldn't of cared.

Sometimes, though, Dad stayed home and worked and then we wouldn't be on welfare. He'd buy us things just like Ma did when we was on welfare. He'd even take us to the fair and buy us coke and things. But them good times generally ended up with him meeting some friends and getting drunk, and then you could never tell what would happen.

Once he took us to the show, and there was this lady there he got talking to, and he was putting his arm around her and kissing her, which surprised me because as far as I knew she wasn't connected with us in any way. But then I thought maybe she's my nina, because I couldn't see why my dad would be kissing her if she wasn't something like that. And I never knew my nina. So I asked her, and she laughed and said yes, she was my nina, and I must give her a kiss. She tasted sort of like pumice soap and candy all mixed up.

When I got home, I told my ma that I met my nina, and she got mad and said my dad was a big liar, that my nina had gone back to Mexico and died when I was just a baby. She and my dad had a big fight that night. He knocked her chair over backwards, and she fell on the floor, and just laid there crying, and he stomped on out of the house. After he took off, she got up and locked the doors and windows.

That time he didn't come home for a long time. And after a week we got on welfare again, which was a good thing because the new clothes he bought me was getting all tore up. So we got some new things again.

Maybe it was because of having it so rough at home that me and Pedro was always so close. I remember another time before my dad went away the last time, him and my mother had a big fight, I don't know what about, and Miz Martínez called the police. They come and got my folks and took them and locked them up. They didn't even see me and Pedro because we was hiding outside in the bushes being scared about what might happen. So when they didn't come back, we went to the supermarket like I told you and got a lot of stuff. We took it home and had a real feast.

We didn't turn on the lights because then Miz Jiménez would of come over to get us. We didn't want to go with her because of María Jiménez's nina who is sort of cracked in the head and does funny things. So we just laid low and sat on the kitchen floor to eat our stuff. I remember we had cupcakes and candy and green figs. We wished we could of stole some coke, but that's kind of hard to do.

"Jeez, María," Pedro said, "if they don't come back, we can just go on living here like this." Pedro is a year younger than me, and when we was kids he used to get crazy ideas. "We can get stuff from the supermarket every day, and nobody will bother us. We won't go to school, neither."

"Oh, huh!" I said. "Somebody'll find out. And anyhow, I want to go to school."

Pedro got real mad at that. "What you want to go to school for anyway, María? I bet it's that Juan Soto that sits in back of you. I'll knock his block off."

"I hate him," I said. Pedro was looking madder all the time. "I can't stand the sight of his face."

"I bet you want to kiss him."

"I don't neither! It makes me sick to think about it."

"You want to kiss him, and he wants to kiss you."

"Aw Pedro, I don't ever want to kiss nobody but you, so there!"

"I ain't kissing no girls, not even you," he said.

"The hell you ain't!" I figured I would get even with him for teasing me about Juan Soto, who it was true was sweet on me. But I always liked Pedro best.

So, I started scuffling with Pedro there on the kitchen floor. Pretty soon we was grappling each other and rolling over and over, and I could feel him struggling in my arms, and I kissed him on the mouth like in the movies. Then he started to cry.

"God damnit, María, don't you never do old Juan like that," he said.

We both sat up. "Of course not," I said. But I had got the shakes, and I couldn't stop shaking.

By that time, it was real dark in the kitchen.

"I'm scared, Pedro," I said. It seemed like things was coming at us, tables and chairs and all. "I wish I could put on the light."

We was whispering, like somebody might hear us.

"Don't do that, María," Pedro said. "They'd come and get us."

I grabbed his hand. "Pedro, I'm scared," I said again. "Let's go get in Ma's bed and pull the blanket up over us."

"She'd get mad," he whispered. She never let us be in the same bed together from the time we was little. If there was only one bed, her and my dad would sleep in it, and me and Pedro had to take the floor but not together. If she was mad at my dad, I got to sleep in the bed with her, and they had the floor. If there was two beds, I got one and Pedro got the floor. So, we knew she'd get mad.

But anyhow we crawled into her big bed and lay there kind of shivering against each other. We figured we'd go back to our own beds later, but we fell asleep.

The next thing we knew, it was morning and they must've got out of jail because they come in and found us. So my dad beat us both with his belt. He didn't say nothing, he just beat us, and that's the last time I ever remember him beating me because it was just after that he went away again. I couldn't go to school for a couple of days on account of the marks, and Pedro told me when he got big he would kill the old bastard. Only he didn't say it where my dad could hear it of course.

Pedro always wanted to take care of me, and I needed him. That's why it was so awful that this time when my dad went away, he took Pedro with him. We just woke up one day, and they was both gone.

I thought Pedro wanted to go with him, and it made me feel so bad I wouldn't go to school. My mother didn't make me go. I just hung around the house, and she mostly sat on the steps and talked to Miz Jiménez. And sometimes she talked to Miz Martínez—who was not out of her head just then— but later she was.

It was then that María Jiménez and me got to be friends. Up to then I wouldn't play with nobody much but Pedro, but with him gone I started hanging around with the girls. I guess I was about twelve then.

We had some good times. They fixed my hair and learned me to use wave set and lipstick. Up to then I had pigtails, and I guess I looked awful childish. María Pérez used to come around and play too, and we would go over to María Gutiérrez's house some days because her folks wouldn't let her play at other folks' houses. Since we hung around so much together they started calling us The Four Marys.

María Gutiérrez was really called María. That was the same name all of us had, but we changed it to Mary when we went to school, not to sound so Mexican. Only María Gutiérrez, they always called her María at home. She's a very sweet girl, and I feel bad about her marrying a egg like Félix.

Gosh, here I was just talking about us being kids together. And all of a sudden María Gutiérrez is married, and María Jiménez is worse than that, and María Pérez is studying and working all the time. And she loves my brother Pedro, and I, oh, God forgive me for what I'm going to do! Only He won't. So that's just the way it is.

After I'm gone, and if Pedro comes back, I hope he doesn't go with nobody except María Pérez. She's the only one I can stand thinking about being with him.

My dad hasn't come home for a long, long time, excepting once in a while to drive by and get Pedro. But when we was little, it was come and go, come and go all the time. Thinking back, I know my mother got real upset in the early times, but later she got used to it, and I think sometimes would be half mad when he come back. Of course, she never turned him out or said he couldn't stay. She would just make me go in the other room to sleep, and he would take my place. Only if she was mad enough, she would keep me in her room, and he had to sleep with Pedro.

I remember one time he had been drinking and he asked her for some of her welfare money to go to the store to get a bottle. She give it to him, and he took off. After a long time she sent me on down to look for him, but he wasn't there. He didn't come home at all that night, and it was a long time before she heard from him again. He had just took off and went to L.A. When he got out of work, he come back all right.

When he got to staying away more than staying home was when she started going out with other men. At first, she was scared to death he would find out, and she would tell me and Pedro not ever to let on about it, or he would kill her for sure. That really had us scared too. I would wake up in the night thinking my dad had come to kill my mom, and I would curl up against her to make sure she was there. I always had the idea she would be took from me by something awful. Or if I was sleeping on the couch or later—when I had a room—in my own room, if I got that scared, I would go running in to Pedro. I would pull on his arm till he woke up, and sometimes I would get in bed with him until I felt better. But I tried not ever again to go to sleep there, because I didn't want no beating.

For a while I think my mom wanted my dad to stay with her, and she told me one time she was going to see if she could make him jealous and tell him she wanted a divorce to marry somebody else. She didn't really, you know, but she thought it might make him stay home more. But I don't think she ever did do it. I guess she knowed it wouldn't work. He might kill her, or then he might just not care. After he started living with that Lola was when she started doing what she pleased and not being scared no more. She just would go with one man and then another. Honest, I don't know what she did, but she would go out and sometimes not get home till morning or even the next day. She never had no man staying in the house with us, though, like Pilar does.

Just one time my dad come back and called her a lot of mean things about what she done with other men, and they had one of their fights. He grabbed the frying pan and took after her with it and she grabbed up a fork. I was scared somebody would get hurt, and I jumped in between them and tried to get the fork away from my mom. She didn't want to stick me with it, so she let me take it. My dad wouldn't hit me neither, at least not as hard as he would of hit my mom. So, he just stared at her, cussed, then he kicked over a chair, and went out the house. She locked the door quick when he was gone, but I don't think he even tried to get back in.

I think the truth is my mom is a unhappy woman with too many troubles that has made her crusty and hard, but inside she's like me. Maybe she's kind of hurt and crying. And it's funny when somebody has hurt you as much as she has me and hurt you so much you can't stand it no more, that you can still be sorry for them. It's too late now, and if I tried to act loving to her, she'd probly spit in my eye or worse. So, it's no use, but there ain't no hate inside me for her.

She's my mother, and if I close my eyes, I can just remember like it was something I dreamed, her carrying me into church on her arm in a white dress with ribbons in my hair. And she was pretty then, too. I can remember it. Her hair was dark and shiny, and she laughed a lot.

Well, them times is so far back maybe I did dream it because she don't never smile now. Seems like she's a wilted flower and has growed thorns.

I guess I knowed for a long time that I loved my brother Pedro too much. When we was kids, it didn't matter. Of course, you're sposed to love your own brother. And Pedro was always so good to me. He never beat me and never wanted me to go hungry, or to see me cry. He would do anything to make me happy, like lie, or steal, or cop school, or anything. And he was the strongest thing and the best thing I knowed.

Oh, my father was strong, all right. So strong and mean I was afraid to go near him. And anyway, he never cared for me because I was a girl.

My mother says when I was a baby, he was real proud of me and used to carry me around and show me off and buy pretty dresses for me. But I don't remember that, because Pedro was born when I was only one year_old. And after Pedro come, my father never looked at me. For a while it was all, "*m'hijo, m'hijo*" that means "my son, my son" and is the way my father talks Mexican all the time.

I guess if my mother would of gone on having babies, my father would of always loved the new baby and not paid no attention to the older ones. But after Pedro there didn't come no more. And when Pedro wasn't a baby no more, but sort of scrawny and eight or nine, my father didn't pay no more attention to him except to bawl him out or beat him up when he was drunk. Maybe by then he had some other kids of his own with that Lola or somebody. I don't know.

This made Pedro feel awful because he loved my father. He could remember the good times when my dad was good to him, so it hurt Pedro inside to be treated mean. Maybe it hurt him worse than me. Girls can take it better than boys that way, I mean the inside hurt, not the outside. Maybe that's why Pedro was never mean to me, because he knowed how it felt.

He was afraid of my father too, even though he loved him. When my father beat him up, he hated him. He would clinch up his fist and bite hard to keep from crying, only maybe some tears would squeeze out anyway. My dad would laugh then and tell him a hombre don't cry for a little stick on his back. My father didn't know that Pedro wasn't crying about the stick—only generally it was a belt—but about the pain in his heart.

This way, my father not being proud of him no more or taking him around with him, Pedro come over to my side. My dad always did think he was a sissy. It's not true. Pedro can be as brave as anybody and is. But it is true, too, that he never learned drinking and cussing and playing around like the other boys I know, because he was mostly home with me and our mom.

There was that one time when my father took Pedro away with him. I don't even know where they went because Pedro wouldn't never talk about it. I was about twelve then. After a few months Pedro come back. He'd run away from my dad and turned up one night looking all skinny and scared.

My father knowed Pedro come back to us, but he didn't come get him. I guess for him that just showed Pedro was a women's boy, and after that he hadn't no use at all for him until a lot later. It was tough in school too because Pedro was littler than a lot of the boys. But he growed-up to be a real man like he is now, only he ain't tall or have big muscles. He's—well, he's all there, but not big. You know some guys has big shoulders but short legs, or maybe they're all legs but a chest like a wore-out balloon. But Pedro, he's right all up and down—not too much here or not enough there but just right. I don't say that just because I love him, neither, because it's the truth.

Anyhow, in school he would get beat up and bloody if he tried fighting. That didn't make him not fight, because he was scared of being called a girl. Especially since he liked to draw pictures and make pretty things, they called him that. But every time he would get into it, seemed like he lost. I hated to watch them fights, and I used to cry when his nose bleeded. But he got so used to it I don't think it bothered him as much as me.

One time we was all playing softball, and he got hit in the head with a ball that knocked him out cold. I got so scared it was like I got knocked out too, and I bawled like anything. But he come to all right, and then the teacher sent him down to the office to lie down, but I was crying so hard she sent me, too. They had this bed in the teachers' paper room where they had all kinds of colored paper, red and green and purple and all colors.

Pedro laid on the bed, and I set beside him. I was scared to talk, and Pedro was still feeling sort of sick, but I looked at all them papers.

"Jeez, Pedro, look at all the colors," I said. His eyes was still red, but he rolled them around and looked.

"Yeah," he says. Then he leans back like he's dreaming with his eyes open. "When we grow up we'll build a house of some kind of stuff all different colors like them," he says. "Every color different from every other."

"That would sure be pretty," I say. I am scared to say more, because the secretary comes in and says, "You children be quiet now, or I'll send you back to your room." And I am afraid for Pedro to walk so soon, so I sit there and don't say a word. But I count the packages of paper, so many yellow, and so many green, and so many blue—like that.

It's a funny thing but that kept coming back to me in my dreams lots of times. The house of all colors of paper. Pedro must of meant bricks, but in my dreams it's always a house of colored paper. And something always happens to it, like the paste not sticking, and it all gets blew away in the wind. Or it catches on fire and pretty soon is all curled up black and white ashy.

The other night, even, I dreamed like me and Pedro was stacking them colored papers up, and my mom come in her high-heeled shoes and stomped on them, so each paper had holes like nail holes all over. In my dream I said to Pedro, "It's all spoiled now," only when I turned around, he wasn't there. And I kept reaching for him, and the wind kept blowing away them holy papers until there wasn't nothing left but the bare field and me poking around like a old lady with a stick that punched holes in the ground, and I said I was looking for candy.

I felt punched full of holes when I woke up and so empty and lonely like I can't tell you.

Me and Pedro was little kids together, and now the pretty things has blew away. I feel a thousand years old. But I ain't even eighteen yet. It must be awful to live and live and feel older and older. But I tell you one thing, it would be even lousier to forget and not care no more. If I was to go on living, that's what would scare me the worst. To get so's I didn't love Pedro no more, or didn't care what happened to him, or didn't even want to remember our house of colored paper that we dreamed up, or even hurt when the wind took it off.

Come to think of it, that's partly what has happened to me already, and maybe that's what is really the worst thing about my life. I mean getting to the place where it's like a window was stuck up between me and the world, so's I can see people moving around and doing things and saying things, only it ain't no interest to me. I see their mouths moving, but I can't hear what they say, and I don't even want to hear. And I can't feel no heat or smell, no smells through that window neither.

Gosh, my whole life was like laying on the grass in the winter when the sun didn't get warm yet. It looks soft and dry, but you can't get warm on it because underneath the world is a old cold bone. When you get up from laying there you're all wet and cold and you can't remember the warm feeling because there wasn't no real warm, just pretend warm from in your mind.

That's about all there is to tell about me and Pedro when we was little, except how we run away together one time. Pedro had this idea we would pick grapes and get a lot of money. We both used to pick grapes with my mom or my dad, but we never got no money for it, because they only pay the grown-ups. So, this time we run off and thought we wouldn't come back. We walked a awful long ways, and it was in the hot sun too, but we had a pretty good idea where to go. Only when we got there, they wouldn't put us on, because we was too young without no folks.

So, we just had to walk back home without nothing to eat except stuff we copped from the fields. We even pinched a watermelon, and we set by a ditch with our feet cooling in the water and eat the whole thing. I don't guess nothing never tasted so good to me.

That night we got home real late, but my mom got home even later so she never did know what we done. From that we found out we better stick close to home. Only mom didn't bother us too much, being out so much, except to fly out at us, saying what good was we to her, or things like that.

We was about fourteen then when we run away. And it didn't work. But now I wonder could we of run away this year and maybe things of been different. Because who would know if we was brothers and sisters or not?

But when I think that, I think it's just paper houses. And then it all blows away.

CHAPTER FIVE
MARÍA PEREZ: LILACS IN THE RAIN

My folks were both born in New Mexico, but it's funny, they always call themselves Mexican, so I guess that makes me Mexican too even though I've never been to Mexico. And to tell you the truth, I don't really want to go there. People tell me they don't have bathrooms in the houses, and everybody's very poor.

It's not that I don't like poor people. We're sort of poor ourselves. But my mother has a sewing machine and a washing machine, and she's paying for me to go to junior college and take this business course. I don't mean it's a private school or anything. A lot of people think junior college is free, but you have to buy books and paper, take the bus there and back, buy all kinds of things and better clothes. If I was out working and bringing in money, it would help my mother and dad, but the way it is, they have to work to help me.

They don't mind they say, and I tell them when I finish, I'll try to get a job in an office. Or maybe after one year instead of two. My mother says that would be good, better than working in the fields like she and my dad do, and she always lets me do my studying first. My mother says most of all to try to speak good English, and I do try, but the Mexican comes easier because that's what we usually speak at home. It would make my folks feel real bad if I stopped speaking Mexican. If I ever have any children, I guess I'll want them to speak Mexican too. But of course, I don't think I'll ever get married.

I can't talk to my mother now about that. She keeps saying, why don't you have any boy friends? I don't tell her they ask me for dates, and I turn them down. She just wouldn't understand. She never even liked Pedro, and if I told her I love him, I don't know what she'd do. Probably get mad and send me to Texas to my grandmother, and then I wouldn't be able to see him even if he came back. Of course, he doesn't love me, so seeing him would be like walking on knives in a way but better than not seeing him.

Everyone has a pretty good idea he was the one that got his sister in trouble. They aren't really sure, but I am. I even heard from María Jiménez that Mrs. Rendón said so.

I suppose everybody would think I was a tramp to love him anyway. But I don't feel like a tramp, because in a funny twisted-up way I kind of understand. And I forgive him and his sister too, for what they did. Of course, I'm not God, and I guess only God is the one to forgive, and how can I know if He does? But I mean, I don't hold it against them in any way.

María and Pedro loved each other. It's just that simple. I know what it is to love, and you don't look up in the dictionary for a definition, you just feel it. You don't ask permission either, and you don't ask the padre, and you don't check to see if the person you love has all his teeth, or if his soul is right, or whether his blood is pink or blue. It its's hard to explain all this. But when love hits you, it's as though you were socked right between the eyes. No, that's too violent. It's as though some great big hand came and opened you up like an apricot and took your heart out like the pit, and you're glad they did.

That's how I love Pedro, and that's how Pedro loved María, and María loved him. When I get to thinking about it, I want to cry, and lots of times I do. But other times the tears can't come out, and that's the worst, and that's how I feel now. Because when you start to explain, you don't cry. When you cry you can't think, and I want to think now. I want to think about my whole life, and their's, and how things got to be the way they are, and what to do next.

I even don't blame María for what she did, if she did it. But I won't do it too. Even though I love Pedro so much, and he doesn't love me, I don't want to die. I want to live and go on loving. Sometimes at night I think about this, about all the sadness and how lonely

I am. Then I think a tree's lonely too standing in a field with nothing to hold it up, but it doesn't just flop over, and I won't either. I think about that tree with its roots down in the earth, and after a while I feel that I'm that tree, and the earth is holding me, and the water in the earth is running up me, and if I don't just waste the water in tears I can make leaves of it, and the leaves can reach up to the sky. Then I think that's love too.

When I go back and think about my life again, I remember the first time I saw Pedro. He was in the supermarket. He was a real skinny kid, darker than me, with the biggest eyes you ever saw and a lot of grease on his hair, and I saw him stuffing candy in his pockets in the supermarket. My mother would have died if any child of her's did that. I went over and just looked at him thinking what a bad boy he was. Then he held out a tootsie roll. "You look like my sister," he said. "Have one."

I took it. "Thanks," I said. I didn't even think about how he had just stolen it in front of my eyes, and I started to eat it. Then all of a sudden, I felt bad about the whole thing, and I ran away. When I got outside, I threw the candy in the gutter and even spit out what was in my mouth as if it was dirty. Then I felt all good and proper again.

Maybe it's things like that, being such a good girl and thinking Pedro was so bad, that makes me realize now, and understand, and forgive. I was a good little girl because I never had to be hungry. We always had too much to eat, and my nina would try to get me to eat just a little bit more. I didn't mind throwing the candy away because we had a big dish of it at home. When I got to know María Rendón, and she told me how hungry they had to be lots of times, and how her brother stole for her, I felt sick at myself because I thought I was so good, too good to steal for somebody that was going hungry.

I will not say that Pedro was a saint, but I will say he was good, and I would say it until they cut out my tongue because he was good. He is good. I know it the way I know God is too good to shut himself up in a Bible or a church or under a priest's robe and send people to hell for loving.

My folks are hurt because I won't go to church or confession anymore, but how can I tell them it's because I love goodness, not badness, and they shut too much goodness out, over there at the church.

Oh, God, if I am saying things that are wrong, forgive me like I forgive Pedro and María.

Pedro and María Rendón were both in my class at school. Pedro was a year older than me, and María was two years older, but they had moved around so much when their folks were following the crops they never got to school much. Neither one of them did very well in schoolwork, and I don't guess they cared much, either. I always cared because my folks cared;

they would go to open house and PTA, both of them, and talk to my teachers. They can speak English even though we use Mexican at home, so they could understand what was going on, and they were always proud to meet my teachers because I did well. But Pedro and María's mother only speaks Mexican, and she didn't even have a good dress to wear, so of course she didn't go. She couldn't read their report cards or the notes the school sent home, and when it was time for topping onions or picking plums, she didn't see anything wrong with taking them out of school to go with her. So they never did catch up in school. Still they tried when they were there, and since Pedro had an especially hard time, sometimes the teacher asked me to help him.

I'd sit at his desk with him and listen to him read. I used to notice the streaks down his arms and think, why doesn't he wash? He used all that awful stuff on his hair, too. But I couldn't help liking him. He had those big eyes and long eyelashes. I guess if I go on this way you will think I am the kind of girl who is taken in by good looks, but it wasn't that way. I noticed how good looking he was after I got to like him. And I got to like him because of his mouth moving so easily into smiles or almost crying as if he felt everything. And even if he couldn't read a story, when I told it to him, he got the point right off, and always understood the most beautiful parts, the parts that most people don't even know are there. He was really different from the other boys in a way that went right through me.

If you lived in our neighborhood you would understand what I mean. Back at the time I'm talking about, maybe we were twelve years old, most of the boys did two things: they had fights and told dirty stories. They swore a lot, too. But Pedro didn't.

It's strange too because if you knew his father, he was just as mean and rough as any man in our neighborhood. And everybody knew he had this woman he was living with half the time. I guess even Pedro's mother knew. But she couldn't say anything, because after all he was her husband, and when she complained even a little, he would beat her up. She would say afterwards that it showed how much he loved her, but that's the way women used to think.

Personally, if I were married—which I don't suppose I will ever be, so it's safe to talk about—I would never let any husband beat me a second time because I just wouldn't be there to beat. But if any of us girls talk this way, the boys laugh and say they will get themselves a wife from Mexico, because girls there still know how to keep a man happy. If that is keeping a man happy, they can have it.

Still, I don't think Pedro would ever beat his wife. He never was mean to his sister. I know because I was around them for seven or eight years, and you may not believe it, but they never had a fight. That boy was always as kind as could be.

I find myself thinking how sad it is that they couldn't just get married. It would have broken my heart, but it is broken anyway. And Pedro and María would have been the happiest couple in the world, all sweet and gentle. Their house would have been like a birdhouse with yellow sun coming in and singing all the time. Pedro could never do too much for María, and María never got tired of being with Pedro. I know they say it's a sin, but why is it a sin? Sometimes I'm so wild and bad that I get to thinking the only sins are cruelty and meanness, and that virtue is being kind and that all the other things don't matter.

I guess I can just never go to confession again. I would have so much to say, I would have to make a recording and let the padre play it over in installments like a radio serial. And I would have to say so many Hail Marys, I would have to put that on a recording too.

If you think I am joking, you don't know how I am crying inside.

I didn't start loving Pedro when we were twelve, but to tell the truth I don't know just when it was. It opened slowly, like a flower, and I couldn't even hear it or see it move. At twelve —he was thirteen—I was just beginning to grow up a little, to strain in my dresses across the chest, but I didn't think about boys. I thought about helping my mother at home and about getting lessons done. I think I was pretty much like most girls with not too many wild ideas or anything like that.

I wonder now how I was so happy with so little to think about. I mean a school party was a big thing, or staying all night with María Rendón, or doing a report, or just spending a Saturday helping my mother can peaches. I didn't ask much of the world, maybe because the world had given me so much.

Pedro was the one wild thing I knew. Not wild like *Los Norteños* but like it would be if you found a wild bird with rings around its neck, or a strange dog you could love but never get him to mind you. Maybe he was wonderful to me just because he was strange.

Of course, we used to go out working in the fields in the summer too, or on Saturdays. We made a big picnic of it. And afterwards I got some money from my dad for the work I had done. I liked the smell of the earth and the fruit, and I liked the dark feel of the ground in the shade after you'd been out in the white dry sun. But I never had to work like Pedro and María had. I never had anybody beat me to make me work.

Pedro used to talk about other things that seemed wild to me like stealing money out of his dad's wallet when he was drunk and then gambling with it. As he said, "I almost won a dollar from that hombre." Just a little kid he was too, gambling away stolen money because he almost won.

If I had a little boy—but I guess I never will—I

would take him to work in the fields too because it's good work. It's good having your hands in the dirt and smelling the tomatoes. It's even good getting your back tired and the feel of resting when you hurt all over. Nobody who doesn't know that kind of tiredness really knows what rest is.

But I would never let it be a mean, cruel thing with drinking and gambling and beating. Life isn't made for that, is it?

I can remember all kinds of things about me and María and Pedro when we were younger, memories that come washing up like waves over me, over and over. The memories are mixed up, but they seem like waves, to be always the same even though some might be when I was twelve and some when I was fifteen or seventeen. It's a little like a song, our life, with a chorus you keep coming back to. Each verse is different, but the chorus is always the same.

Once a really long time ago we were playing ball, and Pedro got hurt. I think a ball hit his head, and he fell down on the grass. He was knocked out cold. I was standing near him, and I heard the ball whizz in the air, then hit him with a whack, and I saw him keel over on the grass. And the next thing was his sister running up to him and crying and crying. But the thing I remember most is the awful uncrying cold feeling I got that he must be dead, and I wasn't even important enough to him to be able to cry. Of course, he wasn't dead. I was only about eleven then and easily scared. But that awful feeling of something grabbing onto me, a grief I couldn't talk about or express in any way — that's come back over and over.

When I was a kid, I loved Pedro the way kids love. Later, I loved him the way a woman loves. And I don't know at all when the one thing grew into the other. I just know it was wonderful and it hurt all the way through, all those years.

No matter how much you love someone though, you can still ask questions about it in your mind. And I ask myself now, how did it happen I loved him? His folks are pretty low people. I like his mother all right, and I love his sister. But they are on welfare most of the time, and his mother has all these boyfriends, and his folks don't speak any English. And Pedro, and María too, never did well in school, and talk bad English, while I try all the time to use the right words and all that.

And even while I say this, I feel like scum, and I know what a cheap lousy thing it is to think you are better than somebody else. A nice girl — oh, I'm a nice girl. No thief like Pedro, no prostitute like María Jiménez, and not simple-minded like María Gutiérrez either. Oh, no, I'm better than them, I mean they.

I could laugh and laugh at all that and cry and cry, because I love Pedro, you see. And for Pedro I would steal, and I would lie down with him in the gutter, and I would follow him around like a sheep. I know it but nobody else does. Oh, they know I love him. It's written all over me in great big letters, I guess. But they don't know how much I love him, and how could anyone know that?

Sometimes at night, all these years, I'd be lying in bed and I'd look out the window up at the sky that wasn't ever completely dark, because of the stars and the lights of the town. I'd think, I'm lying here, and he is so close, lying in his bed. I would want so much to get up and just go to him; I'd dig my hands into the sides of the mattress and go tense all over and almost stop breathing, wanting him so much. Then the hopelessness of it all would come over me, and I would feel slow hot tears coming into my eyes and hurting them, like vinegar, and I'd say, "María Pérez, you stupid, stupid fool, give it up, forget him, love somebody else, but don't love Pedro."

Then the tears that seemed to have made a way for themselves into my eyes would go on coming because now I wasn't crying any more about not having him. That pain would go away, but a new one would come—the sorrow of even thinking of not loving him anymore.

Finally, that would go away too because I'd think, but I do love him, and that's wonderful. Some peacefulness and joy would make my tight muscles go soft, and I'd look up at the stars coming out, and say, "María Pérez, you blessed fool to be crying when you are lucky enough to love somebody." And I'd promise myself to stay happy about it from then on.

Only pretty soon, probably the next day or at most the day after that, the desire would come up in me again, the terrible wanting that tore through me like a storm. And I would have to fight it down all over again.

I fought this battle day after day. I feel as if I've been fighting it all my life. I know now I can't win. Love and desire go together, and unless you're a saint you feel them together. Maybe even for saints it's hard. I have never found a way to love without wanting.

Well, one thing all these battles inside myself did, those nights when I couldn't sleep and twisted-up days—they made me not afraid of things. After how much I've wanted Pedro, what else could hurt me much? Chopping off a finger or toe or even a hand would be simple compared with not seeing him since last July, when it's November now.

And why did I love him all those years? I loved him maybe for the very things that put him out of it with a lot of kids. I loved him because he was short and lightly built. He made me think of a new tree in an orchard, or a colt that had just gotten over being wobbly. I saw one once at a farm where we picked peaches. So light and dancy, it seemed too bad it would grow up to be a big work horse.

Well, I can't say Pedro was dancy. But he looked as if he could have been, the way he rolled a little when he walked, as if his feet were feeling the ground and liking it.

Another thing, Pedro was always crazy over beautiful things. He didn't talk about it because boys don't. But once in a while in school you could see it in his eyes, like when a big silver jet went by in the sky, he would throw back his head and look at it as if he was drinking it.

When we were in grade school, he used to draw a lot, mostly birds and things like that—not so many cars and boats like other boys. When I helped him with his schoolwork, I saw them all over his notebook. He wasn't really good at drawing, but he wasn't too bad either. And the bright look on his face when he was doing it, a kind of inside glow as if he was full of buttercups and fireflies! I couldn't help looking and looking at him when he was like that. And if he saw me looking, he'd pull down the shade inside of him so I couldn't see the light. He'd frown and start doing arithmetic—whistling between his teeth—because boys don't like people to see them shining. And I never minded about that because I do the same thing, and maybe everybody does. Funny, isn't it? We're ashamed to show the best of ourselves and cover up the flowery side with a lot of dullness because that's what we think other people want.

Maybe that's what it is to love somebody: You don't even mind the dull shells they put up because you see right through the wall. And because you see what's hidden from other people, the shine is a secret thing for you and very precious.

And I can remember other times, say some long summer day when Pedro and María weren't working with their mother. This was more often the older they got because after a while, being on welfare and being busy with her boyfriends, she didn't go out to the fields as much as she used to when you might say she was still trying to hold her life together.

Anyway, the three of us, Pedro and María and I, and sometimes one or both of the other Marías would go out to the levee. It would be hot, very hot in the sun, and by the time we got there we'd be glad to sit down in the stickery yellow grass just as if there was shade. And we'd talk and fool around sometimes for hours. Maybe watching a cat hunting for mice in the grass or trying to catch frogs. Pedro was the quickest at catching them, and he'd tease us girls a little, holding the frog at us to make us scream. I hate slimy old things. But he never teased much. María Jiménez was the one that could face him out. Even if he caught a snake she wouldn't be scared and would act like she was going to grab it from him. Then he'd drop it. He was never mean about it, like some boys who would chase and chase you and not be satisfied until you cried.

But what he liked best was lying on his back and watching the big blue and white jays in the oak trees and the clouds sailing over the blue sky.

When I think of that, it's as if we had never grown up. And I think, oh, Pedrocito, if only you and your sister could have jumped up onto a white cloud like a boat and sailed away, and me with you, maybe we'd have found a place where nothing bad could happen, and none of us would have grown up! Isn't that silly? But I think it anyway. You know, not all a person's thoughts are sensible even if he is grown up. A part of me still wants to ride on a cloud and almost believes it could happen.

When we got a little older, Pedro used to take María to the dances at school sometimes, and I went with them. His mother didn't always know, because by that time Pedro's father didn't come home anymore. He was living with his girlfriend part of the time, and part of the time nobody knew where he was. And Pedro's mother used to go out a lot with this man and that. So half the time she didn't know what Pedro and María did.

María would wash her good dress and iron it, and I would come over and help her fix her hair. She had all this dark wavy hair that she used to do in braids. But when we got in high school, she brushed it up loose, and it really looked pretty. It made me think of a poem I read once that said, 'She walks in beauty like the night.' Her hair really was like night, perhaps a little messy but very beautiful. And she had a soft look about her, María Rendón had. She wasn't fat, but she was stocky and, well, she grew up faster than most of her friends. She was really older, so maybe she didn't grow up any faster for her age, but we always thought of her as being our age. And yet, from watching after Pedro so much, and having him almost like you might call a steady boyfriend, although he was her brother, she seemed almost a woman at sixteen.

My mother didn't favor too much my going to dances, but she thought if I went with Pedro and María it would be okay. So we used to go together.

In a way, though of course he never loved me, Pedro always liked me. He used to say I was the only girl besides María he could stand. Funny, because after María died, I was not the first girl he went to. It was María Jiménez. And you know what she is. Though I have been friends with her for a long time and still am, I guess anybody else would say that proves what men are.

But I have the feeling he couldn't talk to me then because I reminded him too much of his sister. And María Jiménez almost helped him, maybe, to lay something away, to kill something that I would have kept alive.

Why should I even say anything about him going to María Jiménez, or why should I mind? If I started judging him, I'd feel filthy, like when I thought I was too good to steal. If I had been Pedro, would I have done different?

But this is all much later. I was telling about how we went to the dances. Pedro was very nice. Not really a gentleman, because where would he learn that? But he would dance with María and then with me and then with María again. Nobody else ever danced with María. They sort of knew Pedro wouldn't let them. Though Juan Soto was fond of María for a long time, and once he did ask her. I think she might have danced with him, only just then Pedro stepped right in front of him and said, "Come on, María, let's me and you dance."

Then Juan had to ask me. Well, he didn't really have to, but he did ask. Only instead of paying any attention to me, he said, "What's eating Pedro all the time?" I tried to say that Pedro and María were very special to each other.

"That's dirty," he said.

"Oh, no, Juan!" I was shocked. I didn't exactly know what he meant, but it shocked me. "Don't you think a brother and sister should love each other?"

"Sure," he said, "but not that way."

"I don't see anything different about it, only it's nicer than most brothers and sisters."

"You're kind of dumb, aren't you?" he said, and then he just finished the dance and walked off.

Was I kind of dumb? Oh, I guess so. But even now, after everything else that happened, I can't believe their love was bad. And I must be wrong because everyone else thinks it was.

Maybe I have a special kind of blindness, like color blindness, and can't see what everyone else sees as plain as day. Maybe that's what the padre means by "moral blindness." But then he says that God is love.

Oh, I wish there were another God I could pray to for help in understanding this God! Because if I am to pray at all, it will have to be to this other God, since the preacher's God is all taken up and reserved, you might say, by other people who are so sure of what He thinks and wants.

To get back to the dances, I suppose it was then I really started loving Pedro. By this time, he had learned to wash more and didn't wear so much grease in his hair, and he was a pretty good dancer. And he still had those big dark eyes and long lashes and white teeth.

Sometimes when I was dancing with him, something happened inside me so that everything was changed. I didn't think of it as love. It was rather like walking through a door into a new room where the air was a different color—say all gold. Everything had a new light. And my body seemed lighter, it seemed lifted and carried on the air, the golden air. For a little while I didn't seem to be myself at all but some sort of shadow that followed his every motion that couldn't get loose from him. And yet I felt more *myself* than I had ever been before.

Then the music would stop, and even so the light gold feeling would go on, even when he went back and danced with María again. I loved to watch them dance. I found myself wondering, when they dance together does the gold thing happen to them?

Lots of times other boys would ask me to dance, and sometimes I would accept. But I found the quickest way to turn off the magic was to dance with somebody else, so I started turning them down.

One time, María Rendón was sick, and I was surprised when Pedro came over and said, could I go anyway? I was so happy I wanted to burst. I didn't even know why I was so happy. But walking over to the school, it hit me all of a sudden. It hit me at just the exact moment I saw a shooting star skip across the sky and go out, and I grabbed his hand. "Pedro!" I said.

"Huh?" He hadn't seen it. And then I let go of his hand, and I knew just like that meteor going out, I knew everything in a flash. I knew I loved him, and I knew I wouldn't have him ever, and the stars went flowing down my face. I got that wrong, they were tears, but they felt like stars flowing out of my eyes and dying.

"Nothing," I said. And we walked on.

Two people can walk together, you know, and be walking not just in different worlds but on different sides of the whole universe. One can be in heaven and the other in hell, but they're almost touching, and their feet make the same sound on the ground. I was in heaven and hell both at the same time, but I think Pedro was just in the world, like always.

Still, we had a pretty good time at the dance. And all the time I was thinking, I'm a shooting star going over the sky, and I'm going to die and be as if I had never lived. And here it was María Rendón that died instead. Now I think I'll live to be very old. I have the feeling I can never die but will go on and on getting tougher and stringier like an old radish left in the ground too long, because the flowers are dead. And María Rendón is the flower.

When we were walking home from the dance that night, it started to rain. We ducked in under a lilac bush in somebody's front yard, and the lilac bush was all in bloom. Did you ever smell a lilac in the rain? There isn't anything like it. We stood there a long time, not talking. I was thinking, I don't care if it never stops because this lilac bush is a little island we washed up on the shore of. I reached out and took Pedro's hand again. I knew I would just torture myself, and maybe he would be mad. But he didn't pull his hand away. I could feel the hair on the back of his hand because he was really growing up now, and I was too.

"Pedro," I whispered, "it's about the prettiest night I ever knew."

"You look pretty in the dark, María," he said.

Well, that struck me funny, and I started to laugh.

"Close your eyes and I'll look even better," I said, and he laughed too.

"I guess that sounded funny," he said, "but you know what I meant." We laughed awhile, but then neither of us knew anything more to say, so we were quiet. Then the rain died down. The sound of the drops on the leaves went slower and slower, and finally you couldn't hear them anymore.

"I guess we better go," he said. Then he reached up and pulled a lilac flower off. When he shook it loose from the bush, all the little drops on the leaves splattered over us like starting the rain again, but I didn't care. "Here," he said, and handed it to me.

I took it wondering. I still have it, but it's all brown and papery and has got a sweet brown smell now not like the spring at all. When I look at it, I try to think of that night, but it doesn't come back to me. But once in a while when it rains, and I pass under a lilac bush and smell the fresh rain on the flowers, then I remember. It slips between my ribs like a knife, and I want to howl, but at the same time the sweetness is so much that I just stand there breathing it in, and that's when that night really comes back to me.

Pedro never said a sentimental word to me, but I can't help wondering why he gave me the flower. Oh, I could scratch the stars and make them bleed for wondering, but they would never tell me!

Things went on this way with me and María Rendón, and me and Pedro, and me and María Gutiérrez, and me and María Jiménez. I was friends with all of them. When we were younger, being friends had been a lot simpler. Then things happened, first one thing and then another, and one evening you looked around and realized that the whole world had changed. It was as though you were on an island, and suddenly all the mountains sank down into the sea, and the places where there had been sea were mountains. After a while, you weren't even sure that you were the same person, either, because seeing so much up and down changes a person until he can never get back again to what he thought he was.

First, María Gutiérrez run away with Félix who was a bracero and a wetback. This is one thing I have never understood. He was pretty good-looking, but so were a lot of other people. Maybe he was just the first person that ever looked at her. She really hadn't gone around with boys at all. María Gutiérrez is a sweet person. She seems to go around with her hands open all the time for giving. I think Félix wanted somebody who could give a lot.

Félix is not a bad person. He is just from Mexico, and although I call myself a Mexican, I don't actually understand Mexicans from Old Mexico very much at all. It must be very different there, for instance, between boys and girls. They don't date the way we do, and they aren't friends the way Pedro and I were. I would like to say are, and my feelings for him have not changed and will never change. But as I don't even know where he is right now, I had to say it the way I did.

María Gutiérrez was brought up different from the rest of us. Her family lives in the States, but they are Mexican all the way through. That meant pigtails even in high school, and longish dresses for María so the boys wouldn't look at her legs, and no dates ever, and always Mexican at home, and all the rest of it. I don't think she ever thought of marrying anybody but a Mexican from Old Mexico. In fact, she always talked about "when we go back home to Mexico." Even though she had never been there! Her dad has this idea about being a rich man back there. So, in a way I guess he didn't mind about her marrying a Mexican. But a bracero might have crimped them a little because after all a bracero is just a poor working man like her dad had been, and like he had stopped being and didn't want to be again. Maybe he hoped for something better for his daughter.

Still, when a girl gets married it's that much trouble off their hands for the parents, so maybe they didn't really mind. When she did get married, they took her and Félix in all right, which is what anyone would do I think, and they've lived there ever since.

Only between me and María Gutiérrez—she's Mrs. Gomez now—it was as though time was pulling us apart. How could I say anything or even have any ideas about what it's like to be married? And then, what could she know of my heart?

But it's a funny thing. María Gutiérrez—I still call her that even though her name is changed—María Gutiérrez with the kind open hands did seem to see through me. One night after she was married, when Félix was out somewhere, she came over to see me, and we sat on the front step and talked low, so my folks wouldn't hear. Usually people talk about themselves and wait for a turn when the other person stops talking about himself so they can get their turn again. But this night María Gutiérrez didn't talk about herself at all. I think she didn't want to. Maybe she didn't know where Félix was, or maybe she knew and didn't want to know. She started talking about Pedro and María Rendón.

"I think María Rendón's lucky to have a brother like Pedro," I said. She looked at me a long time. I could feel her looking, even in the dark.

"Pedro's a nice boy," she answered. She had a hold of a blade of grass and was swirling it around on the step. "But, María, do you really think it's right for a brother and sister to be—like that?"

"How do you mean?" I asked.

"Oh, you know. Like they was sweethearts. Oh, María Pérez, a girl doesn't have her brother for a sweetheart and looking at him like that and holding his hand and all!"

Suddenly it hit me. I shouldn't have to be jealous of María Rendón, which I had to admit I was. Sure, she loved her brother, but she loved him too much.

Maybe he didn't have to love me. But he ought to love somebody else other than his sister. "Maybe you're right," I said. "I never thought about it that way. But I don't see what anyone can do about it."

"Pedro had ought to go away," she said.

"Oh, no!"

"Why do you say that, María?" she asked. But she didn't wait. "Don't tell me," she went on. "I know."

"You think I'm a tramp?" I asked.

"To love Pedro?" She had said the word, not me.

"Yes, to love Pedro." When I said it, it was as though I knew it better than I had ever known it before. It was like a dam breaking in me, letting the water through, the sweet water, the tears.

"Don't cry," she said, and started stroking the back of my head, because my face was down on my knees so the tears could come out.

"I want to cry," I said. "I never cried about it like this before. I want to cry and cry until it's all washed out of me."

"You silly girl," she said. "You think you can ever wash it out and away? You could cry until the street was flooded and it would still hurt you inside. Don't you know that?"

"Yes," I said, "I guess I know it." The tears started

to dry up. And if you ever cried like that, you will know that the worst time is when the tears dry up and won't come out anymore.

We sat there on the steps a long time, and María went on twisting that blade of grass around, and the ants crawled on the cement, and you could hear the little kids playing in the streets. Everything in the world seemed to keep running, everything was on wheels and going smoothly, except my life. I thought about the little kids growing up and getting married and living in houses together, and having little kids, and it goes on and on. Only my life seemed not to get going, but to be stuck on a siding somewhere like a broken-down engine that had never got started.

Even María Gutiérrez, maybe she didn't know where Félix was, but he was her husband. She had him. Sometimes he would go away, but then he would come back again. And he had put this baby in her body, this baby that was growing every day. She looked awkward this way and beautiful too.

I never could see why people don't talk about how beautiful a pregnant woman is. She is big like a flower pod, and when she walks, she seems to carry treasures. Or maybe she's like those old-time sailing ships all covered over with full sails. A thin girl like me carries nothing, doesn't mean anything.

I couldn't feel so sorry for María Gutiérrez. She had this thing in her. Soon she would have a baby in her arms, and so life would be going on for her, and it would be a little kid playing in the streets.

I would go on being empty. I felt pretty sorry for myself, not her. But I couldn't cry anymore, so it wasn't a sweet pain, just more like an ache you want a pill for. Self-pity is that way: not even a clean pain.

"María," I said, to stop thinking about it, "when is the baby coming?"

"About a month," she said. Then, real low, "I'm so scared!"

That shocked me. My mother always said it was good to have babies. She would have liked to have more, not just me, only it didn't happen. And anyway, isn't it a duty?

"María," I said, "you shouldn't be scared."

"I'm so afraid it'll happen when nobody's here, like it happened to Yolanda, and I won't know what to do."

Yolanda Martínez had her baby in the bathroom, and there was blood all over. She almost died, but she didn't because Mrs. Gutiérrez heard her crying and came over and got her and took her and the baby to the hospital. They live next door to the Gutiérrezes. Yolanda was only fourteen, and nobody knows who the father of the baby was. Maybe she doesn't even know herself. She's sort of dumb.

"Your mother's there," I said. "And anyway, you have a lot more sense than Yolanda."

"But my mom'll be picking grapes when my time comes," María said.

"Don't worry," I told her. "I'll come over every day after school from now on. And if anything happens, I mean if it gets started and you're alone just run over to my mother, or to Mrs. Rendón if she's home, or to anybody. Don't just sit there and get scared."

"Okay," she said. And she seemed to get over being so scared. Or maybe she just didn't talk about it anymore.

After that I used to go over there every day, just as I promised. It did me a lot of good helping her make baby clothes and waiting with her. I was to be her baby's nina and that gave me a good feeling, like belonging to somebody.

And one thing about it, I didn't see quite so much of Pedro and María Rendón during this time. So, when the Fearful thing happened, I was more surprised than I would have been, though not more shocked or sadder, because nothing can prepare you for sad things. But I will tell you about that later.

CHAPTER SIX
MARÍA GUTIERREZ:
BIRTHING

Like I said before, I was scared to have the baby. And the way it turned out, it's no wonder.

I get to thinking maybe it's because of how me and Félix started out. The padre says that was a sin. And if you sin, then you are bound to be punished. Still and all, we did go and confess and do penance, and we did get married in church. That was even before I was big enough that you could tell I was pregnant, though I naturally told the other Marías.

You know, of them all, María Pérez was the one that cared the most. About me, I mean. Of us all, she is the most loving, in the way of doing things for other people. She said to me, "María, I probably won't ever have a baby of my own, so I want to be your baby's nina, and I will love it like it was my own." I was glad she felt that way. It's good to have people that care, especially when you have children. Because babies are helpless when they get born, and the best thing you can do is give them lots of kinfolk to look after them and somebody to stand up in church with you when you name the baby. María Pérez prayed lots of times for me to have a boy. That's the kind of nina a baby should have, one that cares even before it's born and ever afterwards too.

María Rendón was dear to me like my own sister, but she looked at me sad when I told her I was having a baby. I thought then it was because she didn't have no steady boyfriend, and here I was already married. Or I mean, about to be—I always think me and Félix got married that day I walked out of the field with him and not that other day in the church.

That's what I thought then about María Rendón. But now I know she was having a baby too. People say so. I hope God will forgive me for thinking this if it ain't true the poor girl not being able to answer me back. Because who would give her a baby excepting her own brother Pedro? And that would be a awful sin.

There is a lot of sin in the world. But how can you take sin seriously, like the padre saying me and Félix sinned, when what we did was loving? And another thing, how can anything that feels so good be bad? It must come from God. Love, I mean, and sleeping close together in bed, and feeling the other person, who feels so sweet. How can you be mad at him? I only wish Félix would be home every night like he used to be at first.

But if María Rendón was having a baby, then it must be true what people say, that she killed herself.

Oh God, when I think of that my breath stops! That would be not just killing herself but killing the baby too. Who could do a thing like that no matter where the baby come from?

I often thought the baby that's inside me is more important than me. Even if I die let the baby live, dear God! I am just like a dish with a flower in it, and the baby is the flower. When I think of all that now, I want to cry. And that's no good. It just makes it worse. And after all, it's not all bad. Because there we was: me loving Félix and having a baby and half-sad and half-happy on account of things. And María Rendón who must of been loving Pedro, and having a baby too, but not even half-happy, I guess. And María Pérez loving Pedro, which I know she did by her eyes and even by her admitting it, and being not half-happy neither, since he didn't care nothing about her, at least not that way. And María Jiménez, who as far as I could see didn't love nobody but had a lot of men around all the time, and enough money, so you see how it had to of been.

Sometimes I felt like I had growed up too fast because María Pérez was still going to school. She was in her senior year, which I would of been if I hadn't of got married. María Jiménez didn't go to school no more, and María Rendón quit just before she would of graduated. Maybe because of not having no graduation dress, I thought then. But now I think different. It seemed like we was all going to pot one way or another, all except María Pérez. Sometimes I almost wished I hadn't of got married.

But when this thought come to me, I felt real ashamed. What good is a woman anyhow but to get married and have babies? And I was sure having a baby.

And when I think about Félix, I still get that hot feeling. Like I said, when he is nice, he is awful nice.

I think too it must be bad if you are married to wish you wasn't. Like going against God. I'm not sure about that. But once you are married, you are supposed to stay married forever to the same person and not wish for other things. Though you do see lots of people going against that, and a lot of them has their reasons. Like if your husband goes away, and you don't see him for years and years, what else can you do? I even think I would get a divorce if Félix done that, and maybe find somebody else. But I hope he don't never leave me. And I would wait for him a real long time before I done it.

Still, when I think of us four Marías playing together in my back yard—we used to play school a lot, or other kid-games like my little sister still plays— it seemed like we growed-up too quick and me especially. Maybe it happened because I'm even more

Mexican than the others, and my folks always drummed it into me to be a real Mexican, and I don't think that matters the same way to the other Marías.

I know some kids, mostly white kids, that finish high school and go to college too. They must be awful old when they get married, especially the girls, and how can they wait all that time? Maybe they don't feel the same way about a man like I do about Félix. I don't know.

When I was getting close to my time in August, there was lots of field work going, and so naturally my mom and dad went to the fields. My folks are always ready to make money for saving to buy that house in Mexico, no matter how hard they work. I sure hope they get it, and I guess they will. But if they go away, it'll be awful lonely without them, unless we go too.

They used to leave Cristina home with me, but then my dad said she was old enough to work too, so that left me in the house alone all day. I tried still going out working too, but I felt awful big, so I stayed home. I tried to clean house some and cook dinner for when my folks get home with the kids.

My mother taught me all kinds of Mexico cooking, and I can do it pretty good, except I can't roll tortillas with my hands like my mom. I have to use a thing, I don't know what it's called, like Americans make pie with, that rolls around. They come out like cookies. My dad says that they ain't as good that way, but I can't tell the difference. And Félix don't complain. I guess to him it's good just to have anything to eat. He must of been awful poor in Mexico.

I got scared that the baby would begin to come some time when I was alone, and I wouldn't be able to get to the hospital. Félix was working, and he stayed out night after night real late, so I never knowed when I would see him.

One day I was at María Pérez's house and we talked about that. I mean, not about Félix but about the baby coming. I told her how I was scared, and she pro-mised to come see me every day and to try and help me when my time come. Since she already asked to be nina to my baby, I felt real good and not so scared no more.

That's the only time I remember that we talked about María Rendón and Pedro. I had begun to think about them, and it struck me how they was to each other almost like me and Félix and how that must not be right. I said something about that to María Pérez, and it made her feel awful bad. That's when we talked about her loving Pedro. How she loved him, but instead of talking jealous about him and his sister, it was like she wanted to be blind. Maybe she didn't want to even think Pedro could do nothing wrong. I know about that. You want to think the guy you love is just perfect, and it hurts when you find out he ain't. It's easier to just close your eyes.

Honestly, I think it's better like that. If you keep believing in him maybe he will get better. Where if you keep looking for things wrong, what good is that? At least that's what I always tell myself.

But it seemed like the baby wouldn't never come. Maybe because I was so big, and the days so hot and empty.

In the morning they would all go off to work, Félix and my folks and the kids. I would put things away and wash the dishes, and then I would sit on the steps. There was always some little kids playing on the sidewalk, and I would think pretty soon my kids will be out there hollering too. But instead of feeling glad about it, it seemed like I felt heavy and sad. The days was long. We lived on the edge of a row of houses, and across from our house was the field. It seemed like a awful long time since me and Félix got to know each other in that field.

When that happened there was green grass, and now it is all brown and hard. The only flowers are yellow thistles with stickers as long as needles and that sharp. And the sky is white and hard too. You can't see no mountains, though in spring when the air is clear, you can see them—sometimes all shiny white. They tell me that's snow, and I wonder how it can be that cold up there when it's so hot down here in Stockton.

It seemed like time had gone empty, and I felt a

terrible sadness being so lonely. I wanted to be a little kid again, like when we had that Christmas play at the school, and I was a angel. It was the only time my folks ever went to the school, and that night my dad called me María Angelita. My mom had let me wear her blue beads that she has had forever, and I broke them on the way home and cried and cried because we couldn't find them all in the dark. My mom didn't say much, but I knowed she felt bad, and that's why I cried.

I guess life is like that. One minute you are a angel, and all the lights is bright and the music is going loud. Then the next minute you're out on your hands and knees in the dark crying and looking for something you broke or lost. When I got to thinking like this, I would start crying because everything was so sad. Then I would think that's bad for the baby, and I would make myself stop. Only the heavy sad feeling went on. You can hold back tears lots of times, but I never did find out how to make yourself be happy when the sad feelings come.

These days María Pérez come over every afternoon. And one day we was sitting there together on the steps talking about things when all of a sudden I got a big cramp. I leaned my head back against the door and said, "Oh!" It was like I had a bad stitch inside me, but then it went away. "I guess it's coming," I said. María Pérez got all upset. She don't have no brothers and sisters, and I guess she was even more scared than me never having been around when anybody was born.

"You got to get to the hospital," she answered.

I almost laughed and told her, "It takes a long time, so there ain't no hurry." Of course, inside I was scared stiff. I have heard so many women talk about how awful it was. And I know now they was right. But I tried not to show it, just like not letting on when you feel like crying.

Then I asked her to try and find Félix, and I give her the name of his boss. She went in and looked in the telephone book, but she couldn't find nobody by that name, so she come back and told me so.

All this time I am sitting on the step, and I get another pain, and this was stronger than the first. This wasn't like with my mom, that I could remember, because it was coming on faster. I felt terrible.

"Do you think you can get somebody to take me to the hospital?" I asked. "Try Miz Rodriguez down the street or the Jiménezes or somebody. I think I better sit here."

"Sure," she said, and went off pretty fast. While she was gone, I leaned back and closed my eyes. If only Félix was here I thought. Just then I wanted him to come home something awful. I thought if I prayed he might come home, and I sat there and prayed. But it must not of been a very good prayer, because he didn't come.

The neighbors' kids was still yelling and throwing things at each other in the street the way kids do, and it come to me, every one of them got born, and this is how. The day was hot, and I was sweating, and I thought I had ought to take a bath. But I just didn't feel like it. So I went on leaning there against the door and feeling like the whole world had gone away and left me.

Then María Pérez come back with María Jiménez and some boyfriend of hers in a car. I was sure glad to see them. I got in the back seat with María Pérez, and off we went to the County Hospital. I even forgot to leave a note for my folks and only thought about it a long time later.

They let us out at the door of the hospital and went off, but María Pérez stayed with me, and I was glad about that. We went in together, her holding my arm.

Having a baby is hard to talk about because for one thing it's so frightening, and for another thing not even half the people in the world has had babies, because some women don't. It begins—or it did for me—with the smell of the hospital, which is something scary in itself, like metal and rubber instruments and cleaning solutions and people being sick. It's a thick ugly smell that gets in your lungs when you go in and don't leave till you have got away from there. It sticks in your clothes and on the bed sheets and everything.

Then there's the halls, so many you get mixed up, and the sound of people walking in them. And doors suddenly opening and somebody coming out crying or carrying flowers or pushed out on a bed with wheels. There's a lot of things about a hospital to make you feel worse, but there's some good things too—like this China girl nurse that led me off to a room. I wanted María Pérez to come too, but the nurse wouldn't let her.

"Don't worry I won't go away only just to call your folks when it's time for them to get home," María said. "And I'll come in the room as soon as ever they let me." It is wonderful to have friends like that. And if María Pérez ever gets married, even if she says she won't, I don't see how she could not. I want to help her out the same way and be a nina to her first baby just like she is to mine.

When the nurse took me in the room there was another woman in bed there. The nurse done some things I don't even want to talk about. They embarrassed me a lot. But first she put up a screen thing around the bed, so the other woman couldn't see. I was glad she done that. But just the same it was pretty awful.

My pains was coming faster, and the nurse says, "I think we better get the doctor for you." I was groaning each time they come. The nurse run out of the room, and the other woman—she was a sort of washed-out blond—says, "Cheer up, María, it'll be over soon." I didn't like the sound of her voice, it whined like a saw, and I said, "How come you knowed my name?"

"Aren't all you Mexican girls named María?" she said. I didn't answer because I could see she didn't like Mexicans, and I wished she wasn't there.

"How old are you, fourteen?" she asked. I guess this was because of my pigtails.

"Eighteen," I said, and she laughed like she didn't believe me. So I didn't say nothing more to her, even when she tried to talk to me. And I turned my face to the wall so's I couldn't see her. But I heard her when she told me she had a baby boy the day before. I thought, when my boy is born, she'll see she isn't the only one that can have a boy. By this time, I didn't see how I could have anything but a boy, I had hoped and prayed so much, and María Pérez had prayed too. Now she won't go to church no more, but at that time she did, and she prayed real hard for me.

The pains was coming faster and faster. It was frightening, like I was being put in some machine and each time they screwed it down harder and then let up a little and then down harder still.

I wished so much for Félix, and I had some bad thoughts about him—thinking after all he done this to me and now wouldn't even set by me. That wasn't fair, because he was out working and didn't even know I was in the hospital, but your mind gets crazy when you hurt so much.

María Pérez come in though and she held my hand, and each time the pain come back, I just squeezed her hand. She is real tender-hearted, and when I groaned she cried a little. I was sweating too. I remember that. I told María, in between pains, that the blond woman didn't like us. I told her in Mexican of course, and after that María just talked Mexican to me. I could see that griped the other lady, but it served her right, and I hope she thought we was talking about her the whole time.

This didn't last very long though, because then the nurse come in, and they put me on one of them tables with wheels, and took me down the smelly hall, and María Pérez had to stay behind. It gets all mixed up after that. But I do remember being in a brightly lighted room with a lot of people all looking at me. I could of crawled under the table and died, only I felt so awful it didn't really matter. The doctor told me to put my legs here, and to relax, and a bunch of stuff. I was so scared I could hardly do a thing, and he asked me did I speak English? I said, "Yes," and after that I tried to do what he said.

Well, if you never had a baby, you won't know how it was, and if you have, I won't have to tell you. I could hear myself screaming, but it didn't seem like the screams come from me. Only there was one point when I thought this is the end, I am dying and can't do no more—and then the pain stopped, and the doctor was holding up a baby.

"It's a boy," he said. I couldn't hardly see, but it was a puny little red thing, and I thought it should cry, but I didn't hear nothing. Then they put something down over my face.

I don't know how long it was, but later there was the pain again, and the doctor said, "Push, Mary." I thought, didn't I have the baby already? Then all over again the big almost-dying come back, and then stopped all over again.

"Twins!" said the doctor. "A girl this time."

I couldn't believe it. I never even thought of that. I felt bursting happy and so tired like everything in the world was heavy and too much, and I had carried it all to the top of a high hill, and I wanted to drop the world in a well and sleep.

After that I don't know a thing, not anything, until I was heaving over the side of the bed onto the floor, and the blond woman was saying, "Damn shame, María," and I thought she's not so bad after all. Then it gets dark again.

Later María Pérez was by me, and I smiled at her and said, "Twins!" I didn't know why there was tears running down her face.

"Anyway, you got a little girl, María," she said, and I was surprised at that. Then it come over me.

"How about the boy?"

"The boy died." The boy died! It was a wave of black water coming up over me, and I felt a howl start inside me and wash up out of my lips.

"He can't die," I cried. "I wanted a boy."

What would Félix say? That was what I kept thinking. The first ought to be a boy to work with the father, and so people could say, 'She's the mother of a boy.' After that there can be girls to help around the house. But girls are a lot of care, and you need a boy to watch after his sisters so's they won't get in trouble. And when a girl gets married, she's no more use to her folks.

Later, I could think we was six girls in my family, and my dad was still good to my mother. But my dad isn't like other people. And I was so scared of how Félix would feel, I just could hardly think about it. But I was too tired to talk, and I must of fell asleep again because the next time I woke up, María Pérez wasn't there no more. And the nurse had brung my little girl to me.

The first thing I thought was poor *Chiquita*, you have lost your brother without ever knowing him. She was a ugly little thing, and I thought then I guess someday you'll go through all this too, and I pity you. Then from pitying her, I thought how she was mine and Félix's, and I reached out my arms. "Let me hold her," I said.

The nurse smiled. She wasn't the China nurse, but she was somebody nice. "A fine baby," she said. I held her in my arms. Gosh, I have had dolls bigger than her. I looked at her tiny mouth, and little nose, and wiry hands that I give my finger to and she grabbed on. My little daughter. It was a great feeling I had then. I couldn't believe she had come out of me. Then the nurse took her away, and I hated to see her go. I wanted to hold her all day.

Then Félix come in. He didn't seem mad at all, and he spoke to me so kind and loving I wanted to cry. "You know about the boy?" I asked.

"*Sí*, sí, María. It's God's will," he said. "We'll have a son later."

I was so happy then. I thought, it'll be okay with me and Félix after all. Then I thought, I hope the son don't come too soon. I'm so tired now.

So, everything was mixed-up tears and smiles. I guess it's always like that. You can't find all good or all bad. Like Félix can be real mean, but he can be gentle and kind too. Maybe God is that way too, giving you something you want and then snatching it away like He was teasing you, but even when it breaks your heart, there's got to be a reason. But my dad says it's damn hard to understand the reasons sometimes, and he is sure right about that.

The next day I found out about the really bad thing, the thing with no good anywheres in it, and that don't seem to have no reason. Because María Pérez come back and told me that María Rendón was dead. I couldn't believe it. I just laid there and cried and cried, not seeing how it could be that there wasn't four Marys no more. I asked María Pérez about what happened, and she didn't say too much. She just told me how María Jiménez's little brother Stefan found her in the kitchen, and the gas was on. To think he had went down to tell her about me having my baby, and she died without ever knowing!

It looked like she killed herself all right. But the priest says it wasn't a sure thing, and she should have a Christian burial anyhow because who of us could judge her? I am glad of that, because I don't care what she did. If María Rendón ain't good enough to get into heaven, I guess nobody is.

I didn't get out of the hospital in time for the funeral, but I don't think I could of bore it, especially having my baby, and wondering about her.

So now there's only three Marys, and the place seems empty. We look to me like walnut shells in a old box—just rattling around and wondering where do we go from here.

But Félix stays home more now and is real crazy about the baby. Of course, he wouldn't change a diaper or nothing like that. But he is a man, so what can you expect?

I wanted to name the baby María, but he said

that's bad luck, and he wanted her to have a real American name. Crazy guy, he don't even know English, but he wants his kids to be American. So we named her Marilyn.

But growing up is sad, and I can't forget María Rendón that was such a good friend to me all those years and wondering why it had to be her.

I guess when my Marilyn grows up there won't be no more Marías unless you go to Mexico to get them. Everybody will be Marilyn or Carolyn or Susie, and there won't never be four Marys again. When I think of that, I feel almost old.

CHAPTER SEVEN
MARÍA RENDON: HER SONG

Me and Pedro grew up leaning on each other like two horses standing out in a field brushing the flies off each other. We didn't care about other people, not even about our mother. We loved her of course, but she didn't notice us too much after my father went away, and she started going with other men. Of course, she would take us shopping, or maybe to the park, or once in a long while to church. My mother didn't go to church much, only Christmas and Easter and one or two other times in the year. I think she didn't like to go to confession.

I can't blame her for having boyfriends, and I don't. She must of missed my father a lot, even though when he was around he was mean to her. I guess she loved him, and if she felt about him like I feel about Pedro, it was really terrible for her. Not that I would want another boyfriend now that Pedro is gone. But that's different, and I guess I do love Pedro more than my mother loved my father. I think I love Pedro more than I love God or anything in the world. I love Pedro more than my life—God forgive me.

But I won't ask God to forgive me. I won't go crawling on my hands and knees up to the Virgin María like I hear they do in Mexico, because in spite of it all, and probably proving how bad I am, I love Pedro, and I am proud of loving him. If God doesn't like it, then He can burn me in hell, which is what I guess He will do anyway, and the Virgin can stand there with her pasty face and watch. I don't care.

Oh, I must be going crazy to talk like this. But last night I went to the levee, and there was this oak tree that was dead standing reaching its branches up to the sky — like I wanted to do but couldn't. So, I run up to it, and grabbed it around the trunk, and the bark was all rough.

"Pray for me, pray for me, tree!" I cried. I was all alone, and anyway I didn't care. And I lifted my arms up like the tree. I thought, if there's any mercy in the world, I will feel it. But I tell you I felt nothing. Nothing, *nada*, nada! God didn't care, nothing in the universe cared. I won't never ever pray again.

But I wanted to say how it happened, to try to explain. Pedro and I was growing up, and so was the other Marías. They was my only friends, and each so different from the others, and all so different from me. This was before María Gutiérrez run off with that Félix, and later they got married. And it was before María Jiménez went bad, which is what the neighbors call it. I guess that means making love for money. Something I don't understand.

María Pérez was the one I loved best, and I always knew she liked me best too. And I knew she loved Pedro.

Now it's a funny thing that as much as I loved Pedro, I never minded about María Pérez. Maybe because I knowed why she loved him, because he is the most wonderful person in the world. And I never thought maybe she would marry him or anything like that, because I knowed Pedro and me would be together forever and ever.

Now I hope she will marry him and take care of him when he comes back because I won't be here to do it, and I'm glad she loves him so much.

María Pérez used to go to the dances at high school with me and Pedro. She never had no other boyfriend, and of course me and Pedro never thought of going with other people.

There was this Juan that liked me for a long time. He was a good-looking boy, and I guess if it hadn't of been for Pedro, I would of liked to go with him. But if Juan even spoke to me, Pedro got black and mean. And I couldn't stand to hurt Pedro, so I never talked to Juan.

The only time Pedro went with another girl when he didn't take me was one time I was sick, and he took María Pérez. I wasn't mad at that because I knowed he loved me more than anybody. He was sort of gloomy the day after that dance, and I asked if him and María

Pérez had a fight. He said, "Hell, no." But he was so grouchy, he wouldn't talk no more about it. I guess he felt bad cause I didn't go.

But there was another time María Pérez couldn't go, and me and Pedro went alone. And I guess that is the beginning of the end of everything. My gosh, is it only last May? There was lots of roses, in fact everything in the world had flowers on it. And now it's only August, just four months later, and look how sad the world is. All brown grass and dead morning-glories, and even though the peaches and plums are ripe, they are sad too and heavy on the trees like me.

So, we went to this dance together, me and Pedro.

Our mom wasn't home when we left. I had this new dress that done up in back, and I brushed my hair up high. Before we went, I come to Pedro's room and got him to do up the zipper. He give me a kiss on the back of the neck before he done the dress up. "Aw, Pedro, you old lover-boy," I said. Then he grabbed me around the waist.

"María, you are better-looking than anybody," he said. "And anybody that says different, I'll knock their block off."

I turned around to look at him, because by this time the dress was done up, and I seen him looking at me like crying. "You're crazy!" I said. I put my hand up against his cheek that was downy, because we was growing up. And when I touched his face it was like a 'lectric shock, some feeling I never quite had before, and I wanted him to hug me so tight my ribs would break.

"Pedro!" I said. I reached out to put my arms around him, like I hadn't since we was little, but he ducked away and wouldn't look at me.

"Come on, you," he said. "You wanna be late?" And me and him started out and walked over the field to the high school.

It was still a little light, and we could see the other kids on their way crossing the field. Some of them was holding hands, and I thought, it's funny how we're getting growed-up, and little kids that was fighting on the playground it seems like yesterday, now they're looking at each other that way.

But of course, I thought, they haven't got a brother like I got. Only then I felt something strange about it. Maybe we was wrong sticking so close together.

I looked over at Pedro, and he had his hands stuck in his pockets, and he was whistling with his face all pulled up and his eyebrows close together. He looked older than most of the time.

"Pedro," I said, "someday you'll forget all about me and marry some girl like María Pérez maybe. And what'll I do then?"

He looked at me fierce. "Who says I'm marrying María Pérez?" he said.

"Nobody. I just thought you might. I like her real well, Pedro. If I had a sister, I wish it's her."

"What's eating you, María? Don't you like going with me no more?"

"Oh, Pedro," I say, and the tears start coming to my eyes, "I don't like nobody but you."

"Then shut up about me getting married. I'm gonna live with you forever, see?" I didn't answer because of all the feelings I was having, and we walked on until he said, "Or are you thinking about running off with somebody?"

"Don't be a ass," I said, talking that way to cover up my feelings.

We had a real good time at the dance. Maybe talking that way going over cleared things up for us. I don't know. Had I been wondering if Pedro would leave me? And was he wondering the same thing about me? Anyway, that night it seemed like everything was settled between us. I loved him and he loved me, and we'd live together for always and always.

I could almost laugh now, but it would come out tears, to think how happy we was just then and how fast all that happiness went sour. I don't know if other people can put their happy times in some kind of deep-freeze to keep them sweet. But ours that was so great, it was just like milk on a hot day and clabbered up in front of our eyes and went bad before we hardly got a taste.

We left early because Pedro wanted to. He said, "Let's cut out and go home, María," so of course I said okay.

We started back over the field. Gosh, I never seen nothing so beautiful. It was just grass, you know, with some daisies still blooming though it was into May. And there wasn't no moon. But the wind had been at it all day and had blew the dust out of the air this time instead of into it, and the stars looked so big and bright like things on a Christmas tree. They was all over the top of the sky and down the sides with nothing left out. I mean, I'm sure all the stars was turned on that night from the top to the ground. And the ground being so flat, there's a awful lot of sky.

"Man! Pedrocito, look at the stars!" I said, and I grabbed his hand. I hardly ever call him that, it's what I called him when we was little. But it come out just then because everything was so special. Everything was turned on, you see. And I had this feeling about all that Pedro had been to me, how he use to swipe food for me, and wipe my face when I cried. I was thinking all that in the same moment I was thinking about the stars, and how great and beautiful it was to be alive.

I'm glad now I felt that way, once. Now I think the stars are teeth that could bite you, and the ground is just a old bone under my feet. But I say to myself, "María Rendón, if you are eating *mierda* now, remember you have eat roses." That is just between me and myself, but I remember all about it, and I'm glad.

So, Pedro put his arm around my waist again like he did earlier, and we walked home together, and I was never happier in my whole life. It was like the stars was ripe plums only silver, and I didn't have to climb no ladder to pick them, because the sky just bent over and dumped them in my hands, lugs and lugs of stars.

When we come to the house, my mom was gone again. Those days we never knew when she would come home and most times it was morning.

Pedro whispered to me when we went in the door, "Leave the light off, _Hermanita_." That's 'little sister' in Mexican, and it's what he calls me when he's feeling the most sweet toward me, like me calling him Pedrocito.

"I can't see," I whispered, sort of scared because it was so dark inside. And just then I felt both Pedro's arms around my waist and he was hugging me tight like I had been wanting him to.

Then he kissed me on the mouth, and I kissed him back. It was the sweetest thing, both drinking love from the other. It felt so great and wonderful, I can't tell you how it felt, and I didn't want to ever stop.

Then his hands was on my hair stroking it. "María, María," he whispered, all choked up, and then he went on kissing me. First his hands was on my head, then on the back of my neck, and then they went down my back. He was breathing hard, and all the time I just held him tight around the neck.

I guess the way these things happen is one thing leads to another because then his hands was stroking my behind. And I knew I ought to say stop, but I didn't want him to stop. Then he felt my hips, and then he held me by the back, and one hand went all over my belly.

"Oh, Pedro!" I whispered. But he just stopped kissing me long enough to whisper, "María!"

Then his hand was up over my breasts, and I thought I would suffocate—because something come up in me like the river coming up behind the levee in spring. It almost roared in my ears, and I tell you I wanted him to do all these things and more too. My own hands started touching him first one place and then another. And it wasn't a crying feeling or a laughing feeling, but more like being in church when the organ starts roaring, and you can't hear yourself think, but you feel yourself sucked up into the music.

Oh, you can think I am awful to say it's like church, but it was, and as long as I am telling the truth I will tell it my way. You don't have to like it.

Then Pedro unzipped my dress, which he knew how having done it up, and slipped it over my head. I held up my hands for him to do it. And he kissed me a long time and felt me standing there in my slip. And then he took that off too and everything. I was trembling so much I could hardly stand up.

"Pedro, Pedro, I love you!" I said.

"Lay down on the sofa, Hermanita," he told me, and I did. I lay down in the dark feeling the prickly cushions against my naked back and the broken springs. For a minute I was alone in the dark and naked, and I wanted Pedro more than ever against me. I could hear him moving around, and I guessed he was taking his clothes off. Then he set down beside me and put his hand on me. I felt up his arm that he didn't have nothing on neither. He had hairs under his arm and some on his chest but not much, and then I felt down farther. It was like there was nothing to be ashamed about.

Then he laid down on me, and he was shuddering too. I could feel all of him. He was sort of poking me, and I moved my legs to make room for him, and we was both trembling. Then he shoved my knees up and come into me.

It didn't hurt, though I have heard some girls say it hurts the first time. No, it didn't hurt at all, but it felt like the most wonderful thing, like the music in church, and like having been running a long time and finally resting, and at the same time like having been tied down a long time and finally being able to move. Most of all, it was like having looked at Pedro from behind a glass window for a long time, and finally just breaking the window and coming to him and being part of him.

It got more and more wonderful until I couldn't stand the wonderfulness no more, and I thought I would come apart it was so wonderful. And then, like a hand had been laid on us both, it was all over and we was still and peaceful, so peaceful, and we fell asleep.

I woke up before my mother got home, and I was surprised to be laying there beside Pedro with nothing on and a little bit cold. First, I thought I would get up and get a blanket to put over both of us, and then it come over me how awful it would be to get caught by my mom like we did when we was kids. Only this time it was a lot worse. So, I got up and picked up all my clothes off the floor and the chair in the dark. They was laying all over like we took them off in a awful hurry. I took them to the room where I slept with my mom and put them on the chair and the shoes under the chair just like always when I get undressed.

Pedro was still asleep, so I found his clothes too, and tried to make sure I got everything, and I put it all in his room. And I still didn't have nothing on. So, then I come and nudged Pedro, and told him to wake up and go to his own bed. He started up, and then he reached out and felt me. And would you believe it, he pulled me down by him, and we done it all over again. This time it was different though. Like when you have learned to ride a bike and riding just as fast as you can for the fun of it, but all the time it is still to music. Oh, it's hard for me to explain these things.

That time we went back to our own beds for sure, even if we didn't want to, because we was scared of our mom. Even if we was growed-up now, and even if mom was kind of lazy and didn't take much care of us or the house and run out with men all the time — even so, she's our mother, and we wouldn't want to hurt her or make her mad.

Well, that's how it started and that's how it went on. From a night with the biggest stars to now when Pedro is gone away and all the stars have went out for me—not all at once but by handfuls. There's just one star now, or rather three, and that's the Marys. Each one of them is maybe just a ordinary person, but they're my friends and I love them. And of course, my mom too, only I think she hates me now, so I don't say much to her. When she is gone, I try to clean up the house and wash things a little to kind of show her. But she acts like she don't see it.

But these stars is dim, all dim. I can't talk to any of the Marías, and like I said my mom don't care about me. So, what's love? I can feel it, but I can't give it. And if you can't give it, it dies. And so do you.

Everything's dying for me. My mother, my friends—it's like they went away, even when I can see them up close.

And Pedro too.

Of course, I love Pedro and have always loved him and will always love him. But he is a star that has gone out. I want him back in the worst way, but unless my mom let him stay what could I do? Oh, there ain't no hope at all. It's hopeless.

Anyway, that was last May, and we went on that way for a couple of months. I mean the same as always so far as anyone could see. But Pedro was my real sweetheart now, and my husband. Anyhow, that's how I thought of him. And whenever my mother went out, he would come into my bed, or I would go to his, and we would love each other. He was so sweet and good to me. I have heard women talk about men always wanting that as if it was something mean they done to them. And I can't understand it, because as much as Pedro wanted to do it, I wanted to do it too. Maybe even a little more. But that might be because I am a year older than him, or I really don't know why.

We was scared of getting caught because even though we didn't feel wrong, we knew what everyone else would say. It didn't seem fair. Here María Gutiérrez started living with Félix and everybody just talked like they was really married, even if they wasn't. And just because me and Pedro was brother and sister, that made it bad.

I have always wanted to tell the truth, but here you can see what a mess of lies everything has to be. I mean to of told the truth about how me and Pedro loved each other, I mean in a growed-up way like husband and wife, would of upset so many people that we just had to keep still and be liars to make other people happy.

Only it didn't turn out that we kept anybody happy, and it didn't work at all. I begin to get funny feelings, pains in my breasts and my breath come short, and I seemed to have a awful lot of upset stomachs especially in the morning. I stopped going to school. For a while, my mom didn't even know I wasn't going. I would go over and help María Gutiérrez, because she was feeling pretty rocky with a baby coming. And Mom didn't know the difference. But when she found out, she asked me why. I told her I was sick of school and would try and get a job. It didn't make no difference to her. She never did care if me and Pedro went or not. So, after that I just stayed home and fooled around the house.

I asked María Gutiérrez a lot of questions about having a baby, and I figured I was having one. Now I was really in a mess, because if I told my mom she would say why wasn't the baby's father doing the right thing by me and taking me off her hands? She talked kind of rough like this most of the time, but her life hadn't been no supermarket, and she was getting tired of divvying up her check with two growed-up kids.

All the time I was scared to tell Pedro too. He didn't seem to notice nothing, and I worried he would get upset. So, I just kept it locked up inside of me and wondered what to do. In a way I felt mad about having to be so sad and wondering—because the best thing a woman can do is have a baby. And I was having a baby and didn't even tell nobody or didn't even want it. And it was the baby of me and Pedro that loved each other so much. If the world was only different, me and Pedro could have a house of our own, and lots of kids, and Pedro would get a job, and I would take care of the house and be a good mother, and we wouldn't never fight.

If only we wasn't brother and sister! But as we was, everything had to be secret and ugly. I just don't understand it.

I wanted so bad to go to confession, but I was afraid my sin was so bad not even the padre could help me. I knew he was God's agent on earth, like they say, but the way they talk about God I figured even He would of throwed me over too, so what was the use?

All that time I felt sure it couldn't be sinful to love somebody like I loved my brother. And as long as I am being honest, I might as well add that to this day I do not think we did nothing wrong—no more than Adam and Eve before they eat the apple. You can say what we done was like eating the apple, but I think it was more like before that, when they was together, and nothing come between them—no snake or no padre or no God. Just flowers and animals and him and her.

It was like that with me and Pedro, I swear it, those summer nights when we was alone in the house and kept the lights off and went to bed together. That was heaven, and I don't care what comes next because anyhow we had that.

After I quit going to school, Pedro did too only he got a job working in the fields. One day he run into our father who we hadn't seen for at least a couple a years. He had one of his kids with him, a boy named Carlos, and him and Pedro and Carlos went to a cock fight in the garage of some Filipino man, and afterwards they all had a bottle of whiskey.

Pedro couldn't bet because of not having no money. So, Dad said did Pedro want to work with him? Pedro said sure. So, for a while he had a steady job going out every day in my dad's old jalopy, sometimes with Carlos or some of his other half-brothers and sisters. And once our dad's other wife, this woman named Lola, went too. Pedro didn't like her too well, but she kept talking about what a big fine man he was, and he had to act nice because after all she was the mother of his half-brothers and sisters. Lola was not the woman who said she was my nina that time when I was little. I never could keep track of the different women my dad had. But he stayed with this Lola a long time and still is with her as far as I know. She was fat, Pedro said. I never seen her.

When my mother heard about this, she was scared her welfare check would get cut off if they found out Pedro was working, so I couldn't tell no one. I sure did miss him, especially having this secret I wanted to tell him, but I never did seem to get the chance. Or rather when we got some time together, I lost my nerve, and besides we was too busy loving each other.

But one night my mom come home early. She must of been mad already. I think she had a big fight with the fellow that took her out because one eye was swole up, and her lip was puffy and red like she'd been in a fight. I never did find out. She come into my room that was her room too, and switched on the light, and caught me and Pedro in bed together, and in fact he was on top of me.

She let out a howl like I never heard before and went into Mexican words that I never heard before neither. I think they was words like ladies never use, but I guess she is no lady, and besides it shows a lot of women must know all them men's words in case they ever need them. It makes me sick even now to think of all the words she called me and Pedro, and the things she said about us which even if I am being honest, I don't want to repeat.

Then she started slapping. Pedro had got up and

pulled on his pants, and he stood there in front of her with no shirt on, and she slapped him across the mouth while she called him things. And he couldn't hit back because she was his mom. But when she turned around to start on me, he said, "Don't you touch María," and she knew he meant it, so she didn't. I mean she didn't then when he was there. I wish he was here now to save me from the way she treats me.

But what she done, she throwed his shirt at him and told him to get out and go live with his father and whatever bitch *puta* was cooking for him and to not come back.

Pedro give me a look across the room. I was crying and pulling at my mother's dress and begging her not to send him away, but it didn't do no good. So, he went and tied up a bundle of clothes and went away. That must of been two o'clock in the morning.

All that time my mother wouldn't let me go to him. She just held me back, and she is strong, but she didn't hit me or nothing until he was out of the house. I was screaming, "Pedro! Pedro! Take me with you!" But my mom was yelling even louder to get out before she called the police on him.

The only thing he said that I could hear was, "I'll come back for you, María." At least I think that's what he said. Then he was gone out of the house. Those was the last words I ever hear from him, or ever will hear, and now I guess if he comes back, he will have a hard time finding me because I will be under the ground. But I think he won't come back or he would of done it already.

Oh Pedro, where are you? I could stand it. I could stand waiting forever if I wasn't so alone, and if it wasn't for the way my mom treats me. But the way things is, I can't stand it and I won't. There's a lot of things one person can take from somebody else. Like my mom sent Pedro away, and she wouldn't let me out to find him. And in a way, she's taking my baby away from me too not letting me live decent so the baby can live too.

But there's one kind of freedom nobody can take away from me, the freedom to die. If I don't want to live, nobody on earth not even the priest or God Hisself can make me live. And if I ain't afraid of what comes after—and how could it be any worse than what I'm going through now?—then nobody can win me out of this game. Because if you look at it that way, even living and dying is just games, and if I lose by living, I win by dying.

This is the worst kind of way to talk if you still care what people think. But I don't. They can go to hell like I am going to do. Then they will know what it's like.

As soon as Mom was sure Pedro was gone she pushed me down on the bed again, and started beating me like a crazy woman with the first thing she laid hands on that happened to be my high heeled shoe. She hit me over and over till her arm was sore, and I didn't fight back but just tried to keep my arms over my head and face and belly to protect myself. No matter how much I cried she wouldn't stop, and she hit me all over my body. Then when she was all wore out, she went in the other room and flopped down on Pedro's bed and fell asleep. She must of been drunk to sleep like that.

I was so sore I couldn't turn over, and I just laid there aching and groaning the rest of the night. For sure she had broke every bone in my body, I thought. I was thirsty, but when I tried to move it seemed like I couldn't. I must of fell asleep finally because the last I remember it was getting light, and then it was bright daylight. Soon as I woke up, I started aching again.

"Mother!" I called. "Mom! Mamacita!" But there wasn't no answer, and I guessed she was either still asleep or had gone off somewheres.

I found out I could turn over and slip out of the bed sideways, and I stood up and looked in the mirror. I was naked, and I didn't hardly know myself, there was that many red and blue marks on me. I was scared to see them all, ever'wheres excepting on my face, and I turned away from the mirror and laid down on the bed again.

Another thing, I could see in the mirror how my belly was starting to swell up. Maybe she hadn't noticed, but maybe she had. Then I started to cry, thinking suddenly, that's a baby in there, and it's Pedro's.

I couldn't fasten my bra, my arms was so sore, so I left it off. After a while I got my slip on. Then I pulled on my dress. It was too much to get my shoes on, so I stayed barefoot. Then I went over and turned the door handle.

My mother had locked me in. I couldn't believe it. She had locked me in and went off and left me. I couldn't get a drink of water or nothing to eat or go to the bathroom or nothing. I went back to the bed and cried again.

I can't see why my own mother treated me this way. But I think she was so scared people would blame her, she just got panicky and hit out at me.

I stayed in bed there all day, and I must of slept again. I woke up with her shaking me.

"Stop! Let me alone!" I cried out because she was hurting me like anything.

"María, get up," she said.

"I can't."

"Why not? You gonna lay there forever?"

"Look at me," I said. "You done it."

She pulled up my dress and slip and took a good look. Mostly we don't never look at each other, but it seemed like even shame between us was gone. She didn't say a word, she just dropped my dress down and went out of the room.

I could hear her in the kitchen. Then she come back with a open coke bottle and a box of crackers.

"You better eat," she said.

"I don't want it." I begun to feel then this thing that has swallowed up all the daisies and stars and made even Pedro's face a shadow. Not caring is the feeling, not wanting nothing.

"You fool," she said. "Drink it!" She sounded so mad I thought she might beat on me again. So, I sat up and drunk the coke and eat some of the crackers. Only then I had to be sick, so I stumbled into the bathroom and was sick.

My mom never cleans up nothing and I was thinking how can I get down on my knees to mop up the floor. But I done it because if I left it, it would just smell worse. Then I went back to bed.

I couldn't walk around much for two or three days, but there was no bones broke I guess, because after that I got all right again. I didn't talk to mom, and she didn't talk to me. But she didn't go out nowheres all that time. I think she was afraid Pedro would come back.

He didn't though, and after a few days she started going out again. And Pedro didn't come, and I didn't know where to get ahold of him. And I had a new feeling, being ashamed to talk to people. I felt all broke up and alone and like dirt, and especially I didn't want to see María Gutiérrez or María Pérez. I knowed now they would hate me, and everybody would hate me for what I done. I knew it so much I started to hate myself.

But María Jiménez was different because she is not good. I mean she is a good friend to me, but you can't say she is better than me, because ever'body knows how she gets her money from the boys for doing things with them. She helps her family a lot and buys things for the little kids, and they act like they don't know where the money comes from. But they must know.

So, one day—I was still feeling too bad to go outside, though my mother didn't lock me in no more—I seen María Jiménez go by outside, and I opened the window and called to her. She come up to the window and asked, "Where you been all this time?"

"My mom beat me up, and I couldn't go out," I said.

"Jeez, how long you been in bed?"

"Five days."

"She must of really belted you good," she said. But she didn't ask what for. Because like in her family, all her dad has to do is get drunk and he beats ever'body up for nothing at all.

"Was she drunk?"

"I don't know," I said. "She was mad."

"Jeez!"

"Look," I told her, "Pedro went away to work with my dad, and I don't know where to find him. Can you find out what happened to him? He took off before my mom beat me up."

She give me a funny look, and then she said, "Okay, I'll see if I can find him. What'll I tell him if I do?"

"Tell him I want him to come and get me because my mom is too mean." So, she went away, and I didn't see her for a few days. I was really well enough to go out by then, but I didn't want to. I hung around the house and waited for Pedro, but he didn't come.

One day María Jiménez come and told me she couldn't find my dad, but she found out him and Lola and the kids had went to LA to look for work, and nobody had seen nothing of Pedro.

That was a month ago. I thanked María, but I didn't act very friendly, I guess. I was hurting so much inside, and she didn't come back. María Gutiérrez—Gomez—has been feeling bad, and she didn't come over. And María Pérez come over once, but I was in a black mood that day. I told her she was too good to visit me and to go away. She stood outside the door and said, "What happened, María? Where's Pedro? Why won't you come out?"

"Pedro has went away, and I don't know where he is, and I feel kind of sick, and I wish you would leave me alone." And I shut the door.

Why did I do that when I wanted to ask her in and tell her all about it? Why throw hate in her face when I needed her to love me? But how could I tell her what me and Pedro had done? Because as miserable as I was, I remembered how she felt about Pedro. And another thing, I begun to think I would never live through this, and when I was gone who would Pedro have but María Pérez? So, I didn't want to turn her against him. I knew he would never care for her like he cared for me because I am his sister, and we took care of each other since little kids. But I didn't want to spoil it in case she could make him happy after I was gone.

It sounds mixed up I know, but it was all there in my mind when I shut the door. That even if she hated me for being unfriendly, I had not done a thing to turn her against Pedro. Really, I was thinking of him not her.

So, I was alone most all the time except with my mother, and she never called me nothing now but bitch or whore or other worse things. One day she said to me, "I guess you're pregnant."

"Yes," I said.

"Well," she says, "Pedro's baby?"

"Yes."

"So, the welfare people will give us a bigger check," she says. You see she don't care about me or the baby. She don't love none of us not even Pedro. I can't believe it, but I see it's true. When I think of her, I don't know when she got so hard and cold, but I see it has happened.

When we was little and my dad was mean to her, she cried just like I'm crying now. I always thought she loved him, and I still think so. But he has been gone a long time now, and she never cries no more. She gets mad instead, and that's a whole lot worse.

She don't beat me since that first night. But I think I'd rather she'd beat me than treat me like she does now—just hard and cold.

Oh, everything is hard and cold and empty even though it's hot summertime. When I look through the window at the field, I can see how brown it is. No daisies and nothin' but stickers and dirt. In my mind I walk out there, and the thistles cut my feet. There is glare all over so bright it hurts your eyes like fingers pushing them in. Can hell be worse than that field is now? Well, I'll find out soon enough.

Because the more I think of it, the more I know I am going to kill myself and be done with everything. Like I said, it's the last kind of freedom I got. And I want to be free.

I get down on my knees at night in this lonesome house, but when I go to pray, nothing happens. It seems like when I try to think of God nothing comes. Oh, I don't think for a minute that means there ain't no God. There just ain't no God for me. It's like God is a playground all shut up, and I am a little kid grabbing the gate and crying outside, but nobody comes to open it.

God is a church with white velvet floors, and I have got muddy feet, so they won't let me in.

God is something nice and pretty for good people. But He snubs me when I try to speak to Him.

And Jesus is just as bad. And the Virgin María that I am named for. Well, I ain't no Virgin, but was she?

Jesus! I had better do it quick before I say any more bad things. I ain't scared exactly, but there's another thing—the baby.

Oh, Christ! Oh, Pedro! What can I do? Everybody would hate him like they'd hate me, and who would help him or take care of him?

And he's all I got left—this little half-made baby that's in me. I got to take him with me. Maybe he's just a red lump now without no hands or legs or mouth. I don't know. When I go to hell, I'll take his little half-soul in my hand, and I'll say to the devil, "Please, sir, it ain't his fault, it's all mine for letting him begin to be in the first place." Maybe the devil will be kinder than people that would call him a bastard—and with him I won't be so alone.

Tonight I was listening to the radio, and I heard this song. I can't remember the name of it, but it was about Mary somebody that killed her baby and got hung for it. But there was this part that went:

> Last night there were four Marys.
> Tonight, there'll be just three.

That set me to thinking. Four Marys—that's what they always called us. And then it come to me like this, and I sung it to myself all alone in the house:

> Last night there was four Marys.
> Tonight, there'll only be three.
> There was Mary Gutiérrez and Mary Pérez
> And Mary Jiménez, and me.

The more I sung it, the sadder I got. I kept adding more lines because now I had turned the radio off. And it seemed like I had got a voice again that I had lost, and I cried because I could sing about it, sing to the empty house and the bare walls and the dark hard thistly field outside. Even though it made me so sad with tears all running down, it was good to sing. Like I couldn't die until I had made my song. It ain't a prayer, because I can't pray no more. And it ain't a letter, because there's nobody to write to. But I am going to sing it again all the way through—right now. Just the way I made it up.

I have got the windows and doors all shut and locked, and when I finish singing, I will go in the kitchen and turn on the gas and think about Pedro,

and pretty soon I will be free and shut off the whole
damn world and stars and all.

So, here is the song, and that is the last anybody
will get from me. The last damn thing.

> Last night there was four Marys.
> Tonight, there'll only be three.
> There was Mary Gutiérrez and Mary Pérez,
> And Mary Jiménez, and me.
>
> Ay! Mary is a good name,
> But why did they name us all
> For Mary the mother of Jesus God?
> We ain't like her at all.
>
> And loving is a wild horse
> That's cooped up in a field,
> And girls is like the green grass.
> They only give and yield.
>
> I loved my brother Pedro,
> And Pedro he loved me
> More than the stars that litter the sky
> Or red plums in a tree.
>
> The stars is like a field of beans.
> The world is like a man

That picks them for a dollar a lug
And takes them in to can.

Last night there was four Marys.
But the saddest one is me.
I made with a man I cannot have
A baby that cannot be.

They'll tell it up and down the town,
They'll tell it in the bars,
And all the kids that's making out
In porches and fields and cars.

The ones that walk and the ones that talk
And thinks that they has known.
What in the hell do they know so well
Of the pain of Mary Rendón?

My life is like the green corn
That's broken by the rain
Until the leaves fall down around
The heart of rotten grain.

My life is like the red plum
Blown crazy to the ground,
Never ripe and never ate
And never made a sound.

My life is like a white moth

That's burnt against the sun.
My wings are turning inky black
And all the light is gone.

Last night you seen four Marys.
Tonight, just look for three:
Mary Gutiérrez and Mary Pérez
And Mary Jiménez. Not me.

CHAPTER EIGHT
MARÍA JIMENEZ: FATE

I could see there was something going on at Rendón's house. Maybe because of living like I do I could see it in María's eyes and Pedro's too. And then Miz Rendón wasn't hardly there at all.

They was sleeping together sure as anything. I knowed it. Of course, it don't make no difference to me who goes to bed with who. Sometimes even I got a little feeling like somebody had twanged a guitar string inside me and made something ring. They really love each other, them two, I thought. And I wondered if I would ever care about somebody that way, but I guessed I wouldn't. Because how can you love somebody if you are charging him so much a time? I thought I must be getting soft to even think about things like loving. Still, I thought about it.

Maybe I loved Pedro too. Just a *poquito*—a little bit. Not like his sister loved him, or like María Pérez did. But you'll see from what I tell you that I must of been that way about him without hardly knowing it.

Anyways, I didn't see none of the Rendóns for a while, and one day I was walking past their house and

María calls me from the window. Then she tells me her mom had beat her up and Pedro had went away with her dad, and would I find Pedro and tell him to come and get her? I thought there was something funny about the whole deal, but I didn't ask.

So, I went looking for Mr. Rendón. He lived in this shack out east of town with Lola Rivera, and they had a bunch of kids, but I don't think they was all his. I got a boy I know to drive me out there in his car. We had to ask around, but we finally found the place. What a dump! Tin cans all over the yard and a open toilet out back. But it was all shut up like nobody lived there.

I asked the lady next door. She was out beating a rug. A colored lady. She told me that Mr. Rendón and the whole family had took off about three weeks ago. Then I asked about Pedro, and she said that after they left a young fellow sad in the eyes—that's what she said—had come asking about them, but when he found out they was gone he went away again.

So, I went back and told María that. And she just thanks me and goes inside and don't seem like she even wants to see me. I am pretty mad about that after all the trouble I went to. So I don't bother her no more.

Now I feel awful about it. Really awful. To think it was the last time I seen her, and I went off mad. And I always loved that kid, even when her mom and mine used to get in these fights, or between fights when her mom and dad was into it, and her and Pedro used to come over and sleep on our kitchen floor. María was sweet and not mean like me. And her and her brother was so close it was pitiful to see.

Well, but the next thing that happened was about María Gutiérrez—now Gomez—and her babies. Her and Félix had not been together more than a year, and they had got married in church just after Easter. That's one time I did go to church. María looked real pretty even if she was five months pregnant. She was always on the fat side, so she didn't look much different from ever.

She wasn't too well, and María Pérez used to go stay with her a lot. And one day María Pérez comes running to my door all out of breath and says María Gutiérrez has got to go to the hospital right now, and did I know somebody that could take her because her folks are picking grapes and nobody knowed where Félix was.

It so happened I had a friend there, Ricardo. He had just come, my folks being gone in the grapes too, and had took all the kids with them. And he was mad when I said we was taking a girl to the hospital. He had different plans. So, I had to argue with him about that, but it ended up I said I wouldn't charge him nothing this time if he would please take her, so he did.

She took on something awful while we was driving her to the hospital, me and Ricardo in the front seat and María Gutiérrez and María Pérez in the back. I was glad I have the pills to take, when I seen her like that. I like little kids all right and would just as soon have some of my own, but not if that's how they come.

I really wanted to stay until the baby was born, but I had made this promise to Ricardo, so we left the two Marías at the hospital and I went off with him. And I will say I had a pretty good time even if I didn't make no money. And I had done a good turn for María Gutiérrez, I hope showing her I am still the same friend even if we are growed-up.

That is the only time, except one other I'll tell you about, when I was with a man without getting something for it. Maybe that's why we had such a good time. My flat old heart sort of puffed up and I felt good about everybody. I remember that. But right afterwards things got terrible.

That night María Pérez come to my door. She was crying. My folks was home, and the kids too. There wasn't no place to sit down, so I come outside, and we set on the grass. It was a hot night in August.

"She almost died," María told me. "It was awful. I waited outside and I could hear her screaming."

"But the baby come all right?"

"They come," she said. "Twins. A boy and a girl. And, María," and she started up crying again, "the little boy died."

"Jeez, that's sad," I said.

"If only it'd been the girl," María said. "Because everybody knows it is bad luck to have the boy die. And she wanted a boy so much."

"Félix know?" I asked.

"Her folks went to get him," she tells me. "And María is half-scared to even see him. She's afraid he'll think it's something she done."

"That would be crazy," I said, "knowing how much she wanted a boy."

"But Félix is from Old Mexico, you know. And so's her dad. And her dad never did trust her going to the hospital."

I seen my little brother Stefan playing on the curb, and I called over to him, "Stefan, run down to María Rendón's and tell her to come over here. Don't tell her nothing else." He just went on sliding this car back and forth on the curb like he didn't hear me.

"Run fast and I'll give you a quarter," I said. He started up and run off at that.

I had forgot all about being mad at María Rendón. It just seemed like The Four Marys had ought to be together then, and I thought maybe we could get somebody to take us down to the hospital. After all, we was friends since little kids.

I said something like that to María Pérez, and we was just setting there in the grass talking about old times. The stars was out but small and glittery like little animal eyes far away. The grass smelled good and I was wishing I set there more nights like I used to and thinking being grown up was not so terrific.

Suddenly Stefan comes running up to me with his eyes round and scared and says, "You better come, Mumsie."—That's what the kids calls me. And I could tell from his face it was something awful.

So, I didn't wait for nothing more but went running down to María's house. He took me to the window, and we looked in, and there was María Rendón slumped down over the table, and when we knocked, she didn't answer or nothing. I felt sick inside, or scared, especially when Stefan tells me he has tried all the doors and windows, and it's all locked up.

It looks to me like she's dead, but maybe she's just drunk or sick. Me and María Pérez stand there for a minute holding hands, and I feel cold even though it's a hot night. The stars prick me like pins, and everything seems uncomfortable and terrible.

María Pérez whispers, "We better not break in. We better call the police." So, I take Stefan—who is also standing with his eyes round like holes—I take him by the hand. I am afraid he'll go running around and talking to other kids about it. So, we go back to my house and call the cops.

Oh God, what a night! By the time the cops come in a ambulance, we have got back to Rendón's house, and of course all kinds of people come running when they see a police ambulance. They break into the kitchen, but they won't let nobody else in, and you can smell gas.

Pretty soon one of the policemen comes out for a stretcher, and they carry her out. There's a sheet over her face, so we know she's dead. Some of the neighbor ladies start crying and some says, "Where's her ma?" but of course nobody knows, and somebody says, "Where's her brother?" but nobody knows that neither.

And me and María Pérez just standing there bawling like a couple of fire hydrants, and feeling sick to our stomachs as if it could of been us, and asking ourselves could we of kept it from happening? It's a awful thing when somebody dies that you have known forever or almost. Like part of your life just shutting off that you can't turn on again.

María Pérez took on so awful that I had to get her back to her house, and we stood outside in the dark. Oh, she didn't make a lot of noise or nothing, but it was like a knife was sticking in her guts she looked that struck. She kept saying, "We got to find Pedro."

"Look, María," I tell her, "I tried to find Pedro, and he ain't around." Then I tell her about how María Rendón had told me to look for him, and how I did.

"You should of told me," she says over and over. "I'd of found him."

"Then just try it now," I say, and she don't have no answer to that. But I could of bit my tongue because what if she'd of tried, and then she'd of been gone too? But I guess she had more sense.

We was standing outside her house whispering and could see the light through the front windows. The light made the streaky tears on her face shine like snail tracks. I felt almost as sorry for her as I done for María Rendón and Pedro. "You better come home and stay with me tonight," I told her.

She knows how I sleep in the kitchen, so she says no. I better stay with her. So, I tell Stefan who is tagging along behind us to go home and tell my folks I'm staying with María Pérez, and if anybody comes to see me to say I'm out of town. That night I couldn't of gone with no man if my life depended on it.

What a empty feeling come over us! Miz Pérez looked kind of surprised when she seen me, but she was nice enough, and she cried too when she heard about María Rendón.

"The poor child," she said, "without nobody to look after her. The poor baby!" Then she asked if Miz Rendón knowed, and we told her we ain't seen her. At that Miz Pérez got even more upset, and she up and left to go see if she's home yet. I guess being a mother she knowed how she would feel better than us. I felt ashamed that we hadn't thought about that. But I never seen too much of Miz Rendón since her old man took off because she had so many boyfriends. I didn't really like her too well.

But Miz Pérez wasn't no big friend of hers neither. Still, she went running over when there was trouble, and I think that's being a good person. You might laugh, but I want to be a good person like that who helps people like sick little kids or when somebody dies. I told María Pérez I thought her mother was super and she looked surprised. "People always help other people," she says. I feel knotted up inside at that because I seen some things María Pérez ain't seen about people.

I ask her, "Who helped María Rendón?" and then we both start crying again. It seems like no matter how much we cried we couldn't get the bad feeling out. It would die down and then flare up again, especially the feeling like maybe we had something to do with it. We was her best friends, along with María Gutiérrez, and she never asked us for nothing or told us if she wanted to die. It seems to me that's what friends is for.

Of course, when my *nino* done to me like I already told you, I didn't ask them for nothing or tell them neither. But I was so ashamed. And anyway, what could they of done?

We was in María's bed by this time and I asked her, "Do you think it was because of something between her and Pedro?" I knowed this would hurt her, but I had to ask her anyway.

"Pedro's so good and kind, how can you say that?" she asked.

"We talked about that before," I says, "and I think they was sleeping together." I thought she would get all mad at that.

But instead she says, "They loved each other a awful lot, and maybe you're right that it was like that between them."

"And you think he's so great!" I say. Sometimes I am mean like when I feel bad. She did get excited, but not like I thought she would.

"God forgive me, María Jiménez," she says, "if I ever look down on somebody that loves." That cut into me, and I put my arms around her.

"You're as great as your mom," I say, "and I wish I loved somebody."

"Oh, María," she says, "you got more love inside you than you even know. You love all us Marys, and your folks, and you do a lot of good things."

I begun to cry all over again. "María," I say, "you know I am a whore or if you don't know I better tell you quick so you can hate me."

"Shh!" she says, "Don't talk like that. María Magdalena was like that too. And she's a saint."

I almost laugh at that.

"I guess I'll be a saint too," I say.

Then we hear Miz Pérez coming. Her eyes are red, and she comes in and flops on the bed. She tells us how Miz Rendón come home, and how crazy Miz Martinez from down the street tells her they took

María away with a sheet over her face. And Miz Rendón goes out of her head almost, crying and praying and cursing. "It's Pedro she cursed," Miz Pérez tells us. I look at María Pérez, who is trying to look all calm because her mom doesn't know she loves Pedro. But I know it, and I can see it wrote all over her face in big letters.

To keep Miz Pérez from looking at María, I ask, "How come she cursed Pedro?"

Miz Pérez looks embarrassed and says, "How should I know?" From that I figure it must of been what me and María thought.

As it turned out, when they brought dead María out of the house with the sheet over her, my little brother had just ducked in and snitched these papers laying on the floor and brought them home. He's awful bad to snitch things, and he can't hardly read yet, so I don't know what good he thought it was, but later I seen it stuffed behind the kitchen table.

Turns out it was where María Rendón had set down the whole story and even her song. Like she was talking to herself, thinking her whole life through before she done it, all the love and all the sorrow. I could hardly read it for thinking everyone should be so honest and love so much and be able to up and proclaim her love and face her death and go out singing.

I kept my mouth shut when I heard my mom and dad say that Miz Rendón had said right out that Pedro had got María pregnant, and she hoped God would burn him in hell for what he done to his sister, and she never wanted to see him again.

So I knowed what I thought all along: that what he done for love—and don't nobody tell me them two didn't love each other or I will beat them up—wasn't near as bad as what my godfather done to me which wasn't no love mixed in it. It seems to me that in sending people to hell even God had ought to ask why they done what they done. But I sure ain't asking no padre's opinion on that! He might say I'd get scorched for only asking. Ask the experts, they say, but what can you ask them?

I don't want to talk about the Rosary or the funeral or any of that. They kept praying for María's soul, and she laid there looking all emptied out and waxy, and I wanted to rip up everything, flowers and big wooden box and all, and be some damn fairy god-mother like in the stories and say, "Wake up, María, the lousy world has been pushed back into shape and you can be alive again and get everything you want." Jesús Cristo! I never felt so bad.

María Gutiérrez wasn't even at the funeral being still in the hospital. And nobody had found Pedro, so he wasn't there neither. So, there was just the two of us that loved her best, María Pérez and me. Besides her mother, that took on so awful. I wore my black dress Ricardo give me. He is not such a bad guy. He even come to the funeral with me, and didn't ask for nothing afterwards, which shows some men are not pigs. But other than being glad about Ricardo, I hate to even think of seeing María Rendón that was kids with me going off dead to her grave like she didn't even know it and leaving the rest of us. I hate to remember anything that hurts so much.

It must of been two or three months after María Rendón's funeral that Pedro come back. The first I knowed of it was when he come pounding on our door. My little brother Stefan answered it, and there was Pedro. Pedro yelled over Stefan's head, "María, why is our house all dark? Where's María? Where's my mother?"

I didn't want to just blurt it out, so I told Stefan to let him in. I was going to come at it easy, but Stefan said, "María's dead, and nobody knows where your ma is."

Pedro looked at Stefan and his face got so awful I went over and took his arm and pulled him down on the sofa. My folks wasn't home that day. They had took all the kids but me and Stefan to Sacramento to see my mother's nina that was sick.

I was holding onto Pedro and I said, "Stefan, you run over Miz Martinez's and ask her if you can stay the night." Stefan looked at me like he was going to say no, but even if he is a boy, I am a lot older than him, so he has to do what I say. So, he just went on out the door forgetting of course to even take a jacket, but

Miz Martinez wouldn't never notice, and just then I didn't give a damn about him and his jacket.

And all that time I was holding onto Pedro's arm and Pedro was just staring at the floor. He had old ragged clothes on and was kind of dirty like he'd been sleeping under a bridge.

"It's the God's truth, Pedro," I said. "It was in August because it was just before school started, and it was Stefan that found her."

"Found her? What'd she die of?"

Now, that was the awfullest question, but I figured it was no good lying, so I come out with it. "I guess she must of killed herself," I said, "because they found her in the kitchen with the doors and windows closed, and the gas was on."

I was going to go on and tell him about his mom, but his face got wild, and he jumped up and then he hollered, "Oh, God!" He hollered so loud I was scared, him standing looking around and the tears running down his face. Then he crumpled up on the floor and begin pounding the sofa with his fists.

"God, you bastard, give me back my María!" he shouted. And then he pounded some more. I was so scared I almost wished I hadn't of sent Stefan away. And it was so terrible to see him there weeping and pounding, I don't know what come over me, but I got down on my knees beside him and put my hands on his shoulders.

"They give her a church funeral, Pedro, and she's in heaven now, the padre says." I can't say I really believed it, but I didn't unbelieve it, and I thought it would make him feel better.

But I guess it was the wrong thing to say because he says, "In heaven! You dope, she's in hell. She's burning in hell right now all because of me. And that's where I'll go, and you, because you're a bitch and a whore, and I'm a bastard." And then he goes to crying and swearing and pounding again.

Well people have called me worse, and since it is more or less the truth, I didn't get mad at Pedro. But if anyone else called me that I would punch them in the nose even if it is the truth. Because maybe if they was me they would be the same as me, so they wouldn't have no room to talk.

I went out and fished around in the kitchen and found my dad's whiskey bottle. Nobody but him is allowed to touch it, though my mother hits it up once in a while when he's away, and sometimes I have a swallow myself. I poured a big glass for Pedro and a little one for me, and I come back. He had quit hitting the sofa and crying but he was still on his knees just staring ahead of him. "God is a son of a bitch," he said.

I am not religious, but it upset me to hear him talking like that. "Shut up!" I told him. "Drink some of this."

He took the glass, but he just held onto it and said it again, "God is a son of a bitch to send a girl like María to hell." His voice got loud and cracked up. "To hell with God!" he said. "Let Him burn for her!"

"Pedro, for Chris' sake, drink!" I said.

He looked at the glass in his hand like he just seen it. "Thanks María," he says, and tosses it off. I drank mine, too. Then he did a funny thing. He stood up and looked at me. He looked me all up and down, and then he reached out and grabbed my breast so hard it hurt.

"You whore!" he said, "How much you charge?"

I must of been soft in the head. I don't know what. But as mean as he was talking to me, I knowed it was because of a hurt that was killing him. I felt sorry for him. Maybe that's a laugh, me being sorry for anybody. But I tell you it hurt me too. So, I just got his hand loose from me and held onto it.

"For you, Pedro," I said, "it don't cost a cent."

"Are you crazy?"

"It's because of María and all that," I said. "It's like in the family."

That must of hit him again because he sobbed, just once, and then he grabbed me and throwed me down on the couch and started kissing me.

I was trying to get out from under him, but I couldn't, so I said, "Turn off the light, you fool!" and he did. And he had me there in our living room, and he was pretty rough. But I am pretty tough.

I have had lots of men, but never one like that, him half-crying and half-biting me, and then just grunting like he was fighting me. And when he finished, he fell asleep beside me.

I begin to get cold, so I got up and pulled a blanket off one of the beds and put it over both of us, but he didn't even stir. I don't know why I didn't go off to my own bed and just leave him there, but I felt like he needed me.

You might say I was soft on Pedro, but it wasn't that. I ain't soft on nobody. Only just this time I felt like he was a little kid that needed taking care of. Though that's a funny way to take care of a kid. But as mean as men are, every one of them has his soft side. A girl like me sees that side of men sometimes. In fact, she has to be careful not to see it, or she'll get soft-hearted and that is the end of her. Like me not charging Pedro nothing. It's all right once, but if I did that all the time, where would I be?

A long-time later Pedro woke up, and he got all upset again when he knowed where he was and what he had done with me. But I started stroking his hair. Honest to God, I did that! And I told him how his mother had left and didn't nobody know where she was. That cut him up too but not like María's dying. It seemed like he couldn't believe it, and he kept crying all over again and saying it was on account of him.

"Look, Pedro," I told him, "I don't want to even

hear about it. If it's a lie, you ought to be damned for saying it. And if it's the truth, damn you for telling!"

"María didn't tell you?"

"María Rendón never said a living thing to me about why she done it or if she was going to." I didn't say how his ma had spilled the whole beans, or how she beat María up, because what good would it do now? "Maybe María Pérez knows," I said, "but if she does, she ain't letting on."

"María Pérez!" he said. It was like he had forgot all about her and suddenly remembered like it was a surprise.

"Yeah! Why don't you go see her, Pedro? You know she's crazy over you. Maybe she'll lie down on the sofa with you, too. And for sure it won't cost you nothing there, neither." I don't know what made me talk so mean. I knowed María Pérez wouldn't do nothing like that. It was like I wanted to hurt Pedro and hurt María Pérez. And after I'd just been feeling so sorry for him.

I guess I felt sick with myself for being soft in the head and wanted to prove how tough I was and how I didn't really give a damn about him. And I don't. But it sure made him mad because he jumped off the sofa in just his undershirt. It was getting light so we could see each other. And he belted me one across the face so hard I was afraid he had broke my nose, but as it turned out he hadn't.

"You—you—" and he called me a name so awful that I won't even say it. Then he put on the rest of his clothes and left. And that's the last I seen of him.

I was still crying and holding my nose when he went out the door, or I would of give him back good for what he done to me. But as I never seen him since, I couldn't do nothing more to get even.

I wanted to call María Pérez right then, soon as I stopped crying and made sure my nose was still on straight, but her folks would of thought it was funny me calling up at that time of day. So, I got up and made some coffee and set my hair. And by then I was feeling better.

When it was seven o'clock, I called María Pérez and asked her did she see Pedro yet. I could tell she was real excited at that, so I told her, yes, he was in town, and to come on over and I would tell her all about it but not on the phone.

It's a funny thing about María Pérez, that mostly you tell her the truth. So that's what I did. Mostly. Just the truth, even about the things he said to me. María is a virgin, I am sure of that, but she never even bat a eyelash. She is not really stuck up or thinks she's better than other people. Even me she doesn't turn up her nose at.

I don't know what made me tell her all that. But when I was finished, I said, "So if you still love that guy, María, you can see he is just like other men, and for your sake I hope you find someone better."

She just smiled, sort of a weak lemonade smile, and says, "I don't want no one better. He was hurting, I think. And you did a good thing, María."

I turned back my head and give her the horse laugh. "Are you off your rocker?" I asked.

"I hope not," she tells me. But I see she is really haywire over Pedro, and nothing is going to pull her out of it.

"I told him to come see you," I said. But I felt kind of sorry and didn't have the nerve to tell her how I told him.

"You did?" She got all flustered. "Then maybe he will. Maybe I'd better get home." And she went off then without even finishing her coffee.

Isn't it a laugh or a cry? Loving, I mean. I ain't never loved nobody. But would I take it just laying down if I hear he'd been sleeping with my girlfriend, if I did love somebody? Oh, I don't know. María Pérez is a saint or maybe crazy. But after she went off, I kind of envied her for not being mad if that makes any sense. Maybe it's a great thing to feel that way about somebody. I guess I'll never know.

But Pedro felt awful good to me in bed even when he was rough. And after he was asleep, I was laying there thinking of him when he was a skinny dirty little kid, and I could of cried.

CHAPTER NINE
A LETTER FROM MARÍA PEREZ

Dear Me,

Didn't expect to hear from me, did you? But we need to talk, and there's no one else I can talk to

So here goes.

Two or three months after María Rendón died, María Jiménez called me up and told me Pedro was in town. I felt unsteady to hear it and as if I heard bells. She said to come over, and she would tell me all about it.

I went to her house, and she told me how he had come and cried when he heard about his sister and called God a bastard.

Then she told me this other thing, about how she went to bed with him. Why did she tell me that? As though love between us, between all of us, had got out of control like a flood over the levee, and love or I guess you could call it lust, was rampaging and sweeping away things we thought would stand forever, and love had gone angry in the world.

I guess even love, the good thing, can turn bad. It washed María Rendón under, and it broke Pedro in bits. And now it made María Jiménez turn against me, like she wanted to hurt me.

She knew I loved him. He knew I loved him. I guess everyone knew, and that made me feel like I was standing naked in the middle of the street.

María Jiménez said Pedro would come and see me. I waited and waited. When I asked other people, nobody had seen him or knew where he went. He never came, and I guess he won't.

But at least time is split up into days, and one good thing, you only have to live one day at a time.

In the morning I go on the bus to junior college, and in the afternoon, I come home again. Then I help my mother, and I go over and play with my godchild a while, and then I come home and study, and then I go to bed.

The world is dark like Rendón's house was dark after Mrs. Rendón disappeared. Now it's lit up again because somebody else rented it. But there's no light inside of me. Maybe after a lot of years go by, I'll forget, but the sad thing is I hate that thought.

I look around and what do I see? Stockton! A nothing-place my folks came to and God knows why. Oh, it's got a lot of buildings and people and schools. Maybe someday I could even teach in one of them. But when you think about places you read about, Paris and Rome and Galveston, Texas, I feel like nobody.

Stockton is flat like you rolled it out, flat like a

tortilla. Just now it's November and the rains haven't started so it's brown like a tortilla too. Everywhere I look, just brown and gray. Brown grass and gray sky. There's a little blue up there like a stain of Easter egg color in the bottom of a bowl, but the rest is gray-blue turning gray-white because of the dust.

In the fields everything looks like it's dying. The wild artichokes that had such pretty purple flowers in the spring have withered up and the dead plants all look like they were shaking their fists at the sky. Most of the seed pods even, milkweed and gumplant and jimson weed, most of them have opened up, and the seeds have fallen down or blown away. There's nothing but stalks, so harsh you couldn't walk barefoot without hurting yourself, and black stains from burning the fields.

How sad I feel, like one of them burst-open seed pods and everything has flown away!

The other day I walked out on the levee among all those sad dead things. Even the ditch water was dark brown, and trees and weeds standing in it didn't seem to want to drink.

But you know, the sun started slumping down the sky and the brown grass got gold and colors shined. Even the brown water looked deeper and brighter, and the plants started drinking. I know they did, and birds started singing in the tired old oak trees.

My biology teacher says there's water underground, and that's what keeps the trees alive. And I got to wondering if there's some kind of underground light like at sunset only inside a person that makes brown things gold.

I feel this light coming into me when I think of Pedro, but I have to not think of him. It comes when I take care of the Jiménez kids, and they put their hands around mine and rub their soft little faces on my own, like roses but no thorns, and there's gold over everything.

Do you think the shine could be God? Some better-than-church God that doesn't care who did what or if there's sewage in the river or if I loved the wrong man? Some God that just loves me?

I would never talk to the Padre about this. He would have it all figured out how sinful I am even in my thoughts, and if that is all God can do for me forget it.

The shine tells me that if Pedro never comes back, or even if he comes back but not to me, and even if I'm alone and stay alone, I will be strong enough to plant myself in the earth like a tree and make a life.

Maybe I'll have to work in the fields like my folks, but I hope not because it's awful hard. Darn! I promised myself I wouldn't be done in and be nobody, so I take that back.

Maybe I can work in an office or maybe even teach school. I hurt in my heart because of still loving

Pedro, and I guess I'll go on hurting for a long time. But when you are with children you are so busy loving them that the hurt curls up and is quiet. I could stand it easier if it only came nights because then nobody could see me cry.

Like my abuelita used to say when she was old, it's not that pain is so bad, but pain all the time makes you tired from fighting it.

I am working on my English which is funny because that's my language, but it's not teacher-English. If you are wondering, I wrote this five-times, and I guess it still has some mistakes.

And maybe someday Pedro will get tired of hurting alone. I know he is doing that, like I am hurting alone too. I don't know where he is, but I keep thinking that someday I will look up and there he will be. And everything will be easy because I will just go to him and give him my love which he has always had, and it will be like music.

I won't forgive him. That's not for me to do. I won't ask where he's been because it won't matter. I'll just open up my arms and take him into me, just loving with no questions, no fears, no reasons.

Then we could start over, Pedro and I, with love sprouting around us like new grass in the field when the rains come. We could build a life and make children to stand straight in the sun, and we could laugh again.

****

I hope, María Me, you've figured out that the para-graph I just wrote is one big fantasy. Life isn't like that. Nobody is that pure and noble, and what man would want a woman that was? I'm no baby. I'm a grown-up woman, and I have to figure out how to build a life. But just now the sky is so awful dark. I have to get through the dark tunnel, and I can't know what I'll find at the other end. And that's about it.

María Pérez

GLOSSARY

Abuelita	Grandmother
Bracero	A Mexican laborer admitted legally into the United States for a short period of time to perform seasonal, usually agricultural, labor. The program lasted from 1942 to 1964.
Bruja	Witch
Buenos días	Good morning or Good day. Used as a common, polite greeting
Chiquita	Little girl, little lady. Small, short
Compadre	Godfather
Curandera	Healer, medicine-man, witch-doctor
Flaca	Skinny, thin, lean, scrawny
Hermanita	Little sister
Hijo	Son, child, sonny
M'hijitas	My daughters
M'hijo	My son
Huaraches	Sandals
Migra	Border patrol
Nada	Nothing, none, not any
Niña	Girl
Nina	Godmother (short for Madrina)
Niño	Boy

Los Norteños	Literally the northerners. Slang: various, loosely affiliated street gangs. Latino street gangs with origins in northern California
Novios	Boyfriends, sweethearts
Padrino	Godfather
Plaza	Square, as in town square
Poquito	Little, little bit
Puta	Bitch, whore, slut, prostitute
Serape	Serape, blanket, often with a head hole in center for wearing
Sí	Yes
Tía	Aunt, auntie
Vamos	We go
Vigilante	Vigilante, guard, slang a person or group claiming to enforce the law, but lack the legal authority to do so.

ABOUT THE AUTHORS

Written by Elizabeth Stone O'Neill and Adele Nova O'Neill: a mother-daughter team of retired teachers.

Elizabeth has a master's degree in Inter-American studies from the University of the Pacific in Stockton, California where she taught elementary in inner-city schools. She was bilingual. Adele has a master's degree in education specializing in curriculum and instruction from San Diego State University. She taught high school art, art history, psychology, English, and United States history, and community college art history. She studied Spanish but is not bilingual. Teaching in California, a high percentage of their students were Mexican or Chicanos with whom they were always close.

Both traveled widely all over the world with special emphasis on Mexico, Central and South America, as well as Spain.

Reviews help independent authors establish themselves. Please take a moment to write a review on the market of your choice.

Thanks